7 BREATHS to SLIMMING

Dr Namita Jain is a leading wellness expert, author and entrepreneur with over 30 years of experience in health, fitness and nutrition. As Managing Director of Kishco Limited and former wellness consultant at Bombay Hospital, she has played a pivotal role in advancing both corporate and clinical wellness initiatives.

A prolific author, Namita has penned 12 best-selling health and wellness books and contributed to prominent publications such as *The Hindu*, *The Economic Times*, *Mumbai Mirror*, *Elle* and *GQ*. Her social media platforms feature insightful video conversations with top doctors, including Padma Bhushan and Padma Shri awardees—bringing expert medical knowledge directly to the public in a relatable and accessible format.

Her holistic approach to wellness goes beyond physical fitness, focusing equally on mental and emotional well-being. She has mentored Miss India contestants, served as a nutritionist on the Food Food TV channel, and been a featured speaker at esteemed forums such as YPO and IMC—empowering diverse audiences to embrace healthier lifestyles.

For expert wellness tips and inspiration, visit www. drnamitajain.com and follow her on:

Instagram: @dr.namitajain | @medicalexperts2024
YouTube: @dr.namitajain8537

What the Experts Say

Eating in a relaxed state of mind and practising portion control can significantly enhance digestion and support heart health. In *7 Breaths to Slimming*, Namita Jain highlights the power of simple, sustained states of well-being.

Dr Ashwin Mehta
Cardiologist and Padma Bhushan Awardee

A calm mind is a calm abdomen, and a calm abdomen is key for good absorption and digestion. In this book, Namita encourages a breath practice to activate the body's rest-and-digest response.

Dr Prasanna Shah
Gastroenterologist and Obesity Specialist

In *7 Breaths to Slimming*, Namita Jain emphasizes a crucial physiological tool: conscious breathing. This simple breathing practice activates the parasympathetic system, brings the breath into a natural, relaxed flow, and supports calmer, more mindful eating. A must-read.

Dr Avya Bansal
Pulmonologist and Sleep Disorders Specialist,
Bombay Hospital, Mumbai

7 Breaths to Slimming is a simple yet powerful pre-meal practice. In her book, Namita Jain shows how this technique helps patients pause, refocus, and stop eating at 80% full. It is an essential habit not only for sustaining results after bariatric surgery but also for cultivating the awareness to stop at just the right moment.

Dr Shashank Shah
Bariatric, Obesity and Metabolic Surgeon

As Namita highlights in this book, discipline is the invisible foundation of lasting success. Whether it's rehabilitation, recovery routines, mental focus, or slimming goals, consistent discipline transforms potential into achievement.

Dr Dinshaw Pardiwala
Sports Orthopaedic Surgeon

Pausing for a brief prayer before meals brings a sense of calm. It is a gesture of gratitude for the nourishment we receive and an act of inner harmony. This moment of stillness allows our digestive forces to function optimally.

Subodh Tiwari
CEO, Kaivalyadhama Yoga Institute

Pausing for 7 breaths before eating to support portion control and slimming is a brilliant concept by Namita Jain.

Saina Nehwal
Olympic Medallist and Badminton Champion

Namita's concept of breath and portion control has been truly transformative for me. After reading her book, I started following her approach, and now we practise it at home as a family at the dinner table. It has had a deep and meaningful impact on all of us, including on my eight-year-old son. In particular, I find it calms me before meals and naturally helps me eat less. It also encourages me to eat slowly and be far more aware of what I'm consuming, rather than just eating out of habit.

These are my objectives, and this approach has had a phenomenal impact on me.

Atul Ruia
Chairman, The Phoenix Mills Ltd

The secret to longevity rests on three essential pillars: proper diet and nutrition, adequate exercise, and sufficient sleep. In *7 Breaths to Slimming*, Dr Namita Jain introduces a simple yet powerful approach that harmonizes body, mind and breath to support natural slimming and overall well-being. An acknowledged expert in wellness and nutrition, she brings clarity and practicality to this vital subject. This book is an invaluable guide for readers seeking balance, vitality and sustainable health.

Bharat Taparia
Chairman, Bombay Hospital Trust

Oxygen—or Pran Vayu as it is called in Sanskrit—is the essence of life. Conscious, deep breathing replenishes the body and mind, enhancing energy, calm, and focus. As Namita Jain highlights in her book *7 Breaths to Slimming*, mindful breathing is a powerful, no-cost way to boost health, vitality, and emotional balance—a simple practice aligning body, mind and spirit in the journey to holistic fitness.

Dr Abhay Firodia
Chairman, Force Motors Ltd

7 Breaths to Slimming inspires us to pause, breathe, and reconnect with mindful habits that make slimming a natural, joyful process.

Kavita Singhania
Managing Director, Express Avenue

7 BREATHS *to* SLIMMING

NAMITA JAIN

RUPA

First published by
Rupa Publications India Pvt. Ltd 2026
161-B/4, Gulmohar House,
Yusuf Sarai Community Centre,
New Delhi 110049

Sales centres:
Bengaluru Chennai
Hyderabad Kolkata Mumbai

P-ISBN: 978-93-7646-506-4
E-ISBN: 978-93-7646-005-2

Second impression 2026

10 9 8 7 6 5 4 3 2

Printed in India

Contents

Preface

Inhale.
Exhale.
Repeat.

That's how this book begins—with a breath. Or rather, with seven breaths. This practice begins quite literally with seven slow, conscious breaths before each meal. This simple yet profound method, rooted in both timeless wisdom and modern scientific understanding, isn't your typical diet book. There are no rigid rules, no forbidden foods, no one-size-fits-all plans. Instead, it offers something far gentler and far more powerful: awareness. A pause.

To breathe.

A moment of stillness before the first bite.

In a world driven by deadlines and distractions, this book offers a pause—a return to self, to stillness and to sustainable self-care.

This is your guide to a more intentional journey toward slimming and self-awareness—one breath at a time. It all began with a simple pause I took before meals. Seven breaths that changed everything.

What started as a quiet moment of stillness became a powerful approach to eating with greater awareness and purpose. It is so gentle, so intuitive, it may surprise you. But don't mistake simplicity for weakness—its impact is profound.

Over time, this practice helps you tune in to your body's subtle cues—so you can stop eating just before you feel full. That 'sweet spot' of satisfaction becomes easier to find. And with it comes lightness, balance and a steady sense of calm control.

By taking seven conscious breaths before a meal, you reconnect with your body, reduce impulsive eating, and shift into a state of calm, clear intention. Whether you're looking for a simple slimming solution, are ready to break free from the cycle of dieting or want to regain control over your portions—you're in the right place. This is about cultivating lasting habits that lead to sustainable slimming and a vibrant, balanced life, free from the cycle of yo-yo diets. Yo-yo dieting, also called weight cycling, is the pattern of losing and regaining weight repeatedly, much like a yo-yo.

How to Read This Book

This book is designed to meet you exactly where you are. You can start at the beginning and follow it as a complete wellness journey, or dip into the chapters that resonate most. Each section stands alone, yet together they form a powerful path connecting eating with inner discipline and self-awareness. You'll begin by mastering the core practice, then explore its scientific foundations and diverse applications, which will culminate in strategies for lifelong integration and effortless well-being.

You'll find tools like the 7 Breaths Practice, the Mini Breath, reflection prompts, and journalling suggestions to help integrate the technique into daily life. No pressure—just guidance. There's no 'right' way to begin, there's only your way.

Before you begin, here's a guiding verse that echoes the

heart of this book's message. Read it, reflect on it—or simply let it sit with you as you move forward.

The Magic of Seven

Quit searching far, quit looking wide—
The answer lives deep down inside.
No need to chase, no need to race,
Just find your breath—your sacred space.

Seven—the number, mystic and true,
A rhythm your body always knew.
Inhale peace, exhale the strain,
And feel your power rise again.

Calm your thoughts and empower control,
Affirm aloud, with heart and soul:
'I CAN control. I WILL control.'

Intensity is not a fight,
But quiet fire, an inner light.
Once you choose and start to see,
Slimming flows—inevitably.

No more noise, no need to roam—
Your breath, your body—your true home.

—Namita Jain

Let each breath bring you closer to your goals, your centre, your best self.

Begin with a breath. Let it lead you to balance, to clarity, to you.

Prologue

The Shift Within—A Personal Journey into the Power of 7

I never imagined that one day, my very breath—something I had always taken for granted—would become the foundation for change, not just for me, but for countless others.

My journey began in swimming pools, on racquet courts and in fitness studios. As a former competitive swimmer turned nutrition and fitness specialist, I built a professional life dedicated to helping people lead healthier lives. I've consulted at a leading hospital, trained dieticians across India, coached beauty pageant contestants and spoken at health forums across the country. Based on my knowledge and personal experience, I've authored several books and written columns to share wellness insights with a wider audience. And somewhere along the way, I realized something important: even those of us who live and breathe wellness, including me, can lose our rhythm when life gets overwhelming. Watching this pattern in others, and experiencing it in myself, is what motivated me to create a guide that brings people gently back on track.

Life, however, has a way of humbling even the most disciplined among us. When I stepped away from my wellness profession to oversee a project in my family business, I allowed my dietary discipline to slip. Gradually—and almost without realizing it—I fell into erratic eating patterns. I gained weight.

I lost the rhythm that had once anchored me. And I felt the gap widening between what I knew I should be doing and what I *was* doing.

In that pause, where regret met self-compassion, something quietly shifted.

I didn't crash-diet, count calories or chase quick fixes. Instead, I returned to my breath: quiet, natural and powerful. From that space, I developed a simple yet transformative practice—7 Breaths to Slimming—a method that brought discipline to the table and gently rewired my relationship to food, hunger and focus. It was calm. It was sustainable. And it worked—not just for me, but for friends, clients, and colleagues, who began to ask, 'How did you do it, Namita?'

This book is my answer.

It's not a diet book. It's an effort to return to simplicity—a reconnection with something you already possess: your breath. And it follows a rhythm as timeless as it is natural: the power of seven.

Why Seven?

The number seven wasn't chosen to make the process sound trendy—it's simply what worked. As I delved into my practice, I noticed how often seven kept appearing, even in the most profound aspects of life: seven days in a week, seven colours in a rainbow, seven musical notes, seven major chakras within the body.

Seven isn't just a number. It's a rhythm. A cycle. A sacred code that has shaped nature, culture and consciousness for millennia.

I learned how seven slow, deliberate, intentional breaths could soothe the nervous system, provide a delay between impulse and action and reconnect us with our body's authentic signals. It helped me take charge, not with willpower, but with awareness.

This was never about counting to seven—it was about returning home to a rhythm that had always existed within me.

The 'Power of 7' became more than a simple breathing exercise; it evolved into a framework for well-being—7 Breaths, each an invitation to return to balance.

And the results? Lasting weight loss. Improved digestion. Clearer thinking. A deeper sense of self-respect.

The Why behind This Book

We are living in a society fixated on more. More regulations. More limits. More complications disguised as luxurious wellness.

Perhaps what we truly need is less—less noise, less pressure, less shame.

It's time to let go of the myth that wellness must be difficult to be effective, and instead, remember what our bodies have always known: rhythm, rest and breath are powerful teachers.

This is a return-to-self guide—not rooted in extremes, but in everyday magic. It's simple, heartfelt and powered by a source you already hold within you: your breath.

It starts, simply, with seven. Seven breaths. Seven shifts. Seven breaths towards a lighter body, a clearer mind and a more compassionate path to self-care.

So, if you're tired of hacks, worn out by guilt and ready for a healthier, more positive approach to life, your journey begins here. We're not chasing change; we're creating it. One breath at a time.

The Conversation That Changed Everything

'Wait—you're telling me I can just breathe and lose weight?' She stared at me, fork frozen in mid-air. *'No...you can't be serious!'*

The scepticism in her voice was almost theatrical. Across the table at our favourite café, my friend looked at me as though I'd said something completely absurd. Her fork hovered, a generous bite of cheesecake perched precariously, threatening to fall. Around us, our group of friends fell silent, forks paused, conversations halted. Even the background hum of the café seemed to soften, as if the world itself was waiting for my answer.

'So, you're saying I can eat whatever I like and just…breathe?' another friend chimed in, half-laughing, half-intrigued.

I smiled, gently placing my coffee cup back onto its saucer. I'd had this conversation many times before—and I always welcomed it.

'Not quite,' I said. 'But what if I told you that by taking seven conscious, intentional breaths before a meal, you could calm your mind, support your slimming goals, and regain control over your portions—without having to give up the foods you love?'

This simple practice involves a specific pattern of inhaling and exhaling that settles your nervous system and brings you into the present moment. It's not magic—it's intentional eating. And when applied before meals, it can be remarkably effective. They leaned in. Now I had their full attention. In that moment, I knew: people don't need more diet rules. They need a pause. A breath. A way back to themselves.

Breathing: More than Just Survival

Breathing is something we do automatically—unconsciously—every moment of our lives. But few realize just how deeply the breath affects our digestion, metabolism, stress response, and even our cravings.

Think back to your last meal. Were you scrolling through your phone? Rushing between tasks? Did you really taste the food—or were you just eating on autopilot? Did you stop because you felt satisfied—or simply because the plate was empty?

In our fast-paced lives, we often eat without presence. We eat distracted, stressed or out of habit—rarely because we're truly hungry. And more often than not, we eat more than we need to.

But what if you simply paused before a meal? What if, before your first bite, you took seven slow, intentional breaths?

This practice—7 Breaths to Slimming—is built on three powerful principles: relaxation, discipline and portion control. These 7 Breaths help shift your body from the fight or flight state, which can hinder digestion and trigger cravings, to the rest and digest mode—allowing you to eat with clarity and purpose.

Discipline here isn't about restriction—it's about reconnecting. With each breath, you centre yourself, strengthen your resolve, and return to your slimming goals.

And for those busy moments when seven full breaths feel out of reach, there's the Mini Breath practice—a quick, three-breath reset that brings you back to intentional eating. It's fast, practical and surprisingly powerful.

Ditch the Diet Plan, Keep the Results

'Namita, why aren't you including a diet plan in this book?'

It's a fair question. And here's my answer: because no single diet works for everyone. We're not carbon copies—we have different body types, cultures, preferences and lifestyles. Real wellness isn't one-size-fits-all. This book teaches portion control through the '7 Breaths' technique and encourages intuitive food choices, making slimming simple and effortless.

It's not just about following a diet. It's about embracing a mindful approach to living, understanding the philosophy behind each choice, and tuning into the subtle signals of your body. Just as the number seven appears throughout nature, music, and the human energy system, our journey toward wellness is deeply interconnected—body, mind and spirit. This book goes beyond calories and meal plans to offer a holistic path, helping you align your habits, thoughts and lifestyle in a way that honours your unique self.

The foods we grew up with—the dishes that comfort us, that connect us to our families and cultures—are deeply personal.

In southern India, rice is a way of life. In the north, wheat-based dishes dominate the table. Coastal regions favour coconut-rich curries and seafood, while inland areas embrace millets, pulses and seasonal produce.

Across the world, food reflects tradition and geography.

In Italy, it's pasta. In Japan, sushi. In Mexico, tacos. In the Middle East, Mediterranean. In France, small portions are savoured slowly.

Beyond culture, our daily lives shape our needs. Whether you're a desk-bound professional, an athlete, or a full-time parent—what you need nutritionally will vary.

So no, I'm not here to hand you a list of dos and don'ts. I want to help you tune in to your body and eat in a way that actually works for you.

Because no matter who you are or what cuisine you love, one truth is universal: portion control matters.

Most diet plans impose rigid rules—what to eat and when to eat. But what if, instead of following strict rules, you followed awareness, discipline and inner guidance?

7 Breaths to Slimming offers just that. A simple pause before each meal. A moment to reset. To eat with intention—and still savour every bite.

The Pre-Meal Pause That Changes Everything

Taking seven breaths before a meal may sound too simple to be effective. But that's exactly why it works. In those few seconds of stillness, your nervous system shifts—you move from stress to calm. Your thoughts settle. Your body softens. You become present.

This brief pause lets you check in: Am I hungry? How much do I need? What will nourish me right now? And without forcing anything, the shift begins. You eat more slowly. More consciously. You stop when you're truly satisfied—not just because the plate is empty.

Portion Control Isn't Deprivation

Let's clear up a common myth: portion control does not mean eating tiny amounts or going hungry. It's not about measuring every spoonful or counting each grain of rice. It's about eating just enough—honouring your hunger without overloading your body.

With *7 Breaths to Slimming*, you learn to stop at the point of gentle satisfaction—about eighty per cent full. You feel light, energized and content. Not stuffed. Not guilty.

That one simple shift—eating with your goals in mind, not your impulses—can transform the way your body feels and responds to food.

Portion Wisdom from around the World

Sensible portion sizes aren't a new concept. Many traditional cultures have been embracing them for generations.

In Japan, the practice of *hara hachi bu*—eating until eighty per cent full—is linked to longevity and better digestion. Similarly, in Buddhist teachings, mindful eating is part of a larger philosophy of moderation and self-awareness. Monks are often trained to eat slowly, with gratitude and restraint, stopping when their bodies feel nourished—not full.

In France, meals are savoured with smaller portions and a focus on quality. In Indian homes, the traditional thali reflects balance and variety in modest portions. While restaurant thalis may go overboard, the home-style version encourages awareness and satisfaction.

Since we explored how mindful eating and stopping when one is around eighty per cent full is a common practice among monks, it's interesting to see how a similar philosophy is followed even in the business world. Many successful businessmen, CEOs and Wall Street bankers believe in never making a deal on a full stomach. Leaving a little hunger, they say, keeps the mind sharp, the body active, and the appetite for better decisions alive. Eating until you're only about eighty per cent full prevents lethargy and helps maintain focus and energy, whether for spiritual practice or closing a big business deal. In both worlds, the principle is the same: moderation fuels clarity, alertness and performance.

Contrast this with modern fast-food culture, where oversized portions have become the norm—especially in the West. This leads to unconscious overeating and weight gain.

You don't need to abandon the foods you love. You just need to pay attention to how much you are eating. And that begins with a simple breath.

The Science behind Smarter Eating

Science backs what ancient wisdom already knew: portion sizes influence how much we eat—often more than hunger does. Studies in the *American Journal of Clinical Nutrition* confirm that people who are served bigger portions tend to eat significantly more—without even realizing it. The *Journal of Nutrition* notes that portion sizes have grown dramatically over the last few decades, mirroring the rise in obesity rates.[1]

The message is clear: more food on the plate usually means more food in the body. But the good news is—you can break the cycle. All it takes is a pause. Seven breaths.

---

[1]Livingstone, M.B E., and L.K. Pourshahidi, 'Portion size and obesity', *Advances in Nutrition*, Vol. 5, No. 6, 2014, pp. 829–34. https://tinyurl.com/yxxwsu7n. Accessed on 1 December 2025.

Breathing: A New Approach to Slimming

7 Breaths to Slimming is not about restriction—it's about intention.

Before every meal, you pause. You breathe. You check in. Am I truly hungry? Or just bored, stressed or emotional? That moment of clarity creates space for a conscious choice—not a conditioned one. No calorie-counting. No guilt. No complicated plans. Just breath after breath—seven in total. Long enough to reset. Short enough to stay practical. Until your body speaks for itself.

A Small Habit, a Big Transformation

Over time, this simple pre-meal practice becomes second nature. You eat less. Enjoy more. Trust your body again. Each breath isn't just a pause—it's a practice of inner discipline. Not the rigid kind, but a steady, self-supporting commitment to your slimming goals. As I finished explaining, my friend looked down at her dessert. Then, almost shyly, she took a long, deliberate breath. A real one.

She smiled. 'All right,' she said. 'I'll try it. But if I take seven breaths and still want the cheesecake, I'm going for it.' I laughed. 'Fair enough. But don't be surprised if those seven breaths shift something.' Because lasting change doesn't begin with perfection. It begins with intention—gently supported by discipline.

Track the Shift: A Journal for the Journey

To deepen your experience, try keeping a simple food-and-feeling journal. Track how you feel before and after meals, and how the 7 Breaths align with your goals. You may be surprised by what you discover. So, before your next meal, pause. Take seven slow, conscious breaths. Notice the shift.

'Sometimes the smallest step in the right direction ends up being the biggest step of your life.'—Naeem Callaway

SECTION ONE

Laying the Foundation: Why This Works

This section introduces the foundation of 7 Breaths to Slimming: a simple, calming pause that helps you shift from automatic eating to conscious choice. Backed by science and inspired by global traditions, the practice supports better digestion, reduces cravings and builds lasting discipline—not through willpower, but through presence and awareness.

It's not a diet. It's a habit. And it starts with 7 Breaths.

1

Prep to Digest

'Digestion doesn't begin with food—it begins with how you prepare your body to receive it.'

The Digestive Power of Pause

(Yes, you really can breathe your way to better digestion—and a lighter you.)

Let's set the scene. You skipped breakfast (again), powered through a tidal wave of emails, fuelled by caffeine and willpower, and now it's 2:47 p.m. You're starving. You attack lunch like an Olympic sport—barely chewing, your mind racing towards the next Zoom call. Ten minutes later: bloated, heavy and guilty. Sound familiar? You're not alone. Most of us eat like we're racing the clock, not fuelling our bodies. We inhale food and wonder why digestion's a no-show.

Here's the thing: your body wasn't ready—not because of what you ate, but how you ate. You didn't pause or prepare your body, your nervous system, your digestive fire, your presence. What was missing? A moment of calm. A pause. To breathe. What if you could turn things around with just a few conscious breaths? Before your next bite, pause and breathe using the easy-to-follow 7 Breaths to Slimming method.

When Anxiety Sits at the Table, Digestion Walks out

It's not just what you eat—it's how you feel while eating. Are you stressed or calm? Rushing, scrolling, worrying or planning, while chewing puts your body on high alert. It shifts into fight or flight, and digestion shuts down first.

But when you're calm, something magical happens. Your body shifts gears. It softens. It listens. It gets the message: 'I'm safe now; we can digest.' This is called the rest-and-digest state, and it's where real nourishment begins.

So, how do you flip that switch from chaos to calm? Start with your breath. One deep, conscious breath tells your body: 'It's okay, you're safe.' Seven breaths? A simple reset that wakes your calm and fuels your digestive fire. But the moment you're shovelling bites between emails, scrolling through your phone mid-meal or narrating your life story across the table while chewing? Congratulations—you've locked yourself back in fight-or-flight mode. Digestion takes a back seat, and instead of nourishment, you get discomfort, acidity, flatulence, and yes, a little extra weight tagging along.

The 7 Breaths practice: Not a ritual. Not a gimmick—just science (and sanity).

The 7 Breaths to Slimming is simple yet powerful. First, become conscious of your breath. Most of us take breathing for granted.

Bringing Conscious Awareness to Your Breath

Before eating, take a moment to simply notice your breath. You can be sitting or standing comfortably, perhaps closing your eyes gently to help you focus. Bring your attention to the rise and fall of your breath in your body. Allow your breath to be gentle and natural, without any need to force or change it. Simply observe each inhale and each exhale as it occurs. Take a few moments to be fully present with your breathing before you begin your meal.

The Physiology of Breath and Digestion

Pausing for the 7 Breaths isn't yoga showmanship or a wellness fad. You activate your vagus nerve—the body's communication hero that regulates digestion, lowers stress and boosts well-being. Slow, deep breathing, especially with a slightly extended exhale, increases heart rate variability (HRV)—a key indicator of a balanced nervous system and a shift towards parasympathetic dominance. This tells your body that it's safe and ready to digest.

Cultivating Breath Awareness and Interoception

Beyond the pre-meal pause, cultivating a general awareness of your breath throughout the day can significantly enhance your connection to your body's internal cues—a concept known as interoception. For instance, noticing the tightness in your stomach before stress eating, the lightness that settles in after a few calm breaths, or the subtle moment when hunger gently shifts into fullness. When you're attuned to your breath, you become more sensitive to feelings of hunger, fullness and overall bodily sensations. This supports intentional eating and makes the 7 Breaths method even more effective in tuning you into your body's needs.

Even a brief pause before meals—whether through intentional breathing, a moment of silence or a quiet prayer—

activates this internal switch. You're telling your body: 'We are safe. We can relax now. Let's receive this meal.' With each breath, you calm the mind, strengthen your resolve and eat with conscious intention rather than impulse. That's not hype. That's physiology working in your favour.

The Timeless Wisdom of the Pre-Meal Pause

Long before gut health became a buzzword and wellness feeds overflowed with superfoods, ancient cultures across the world already understood a quiet truth: digestion begins before the first bite.

These weren't just quaint customs or spiritual rituals—they were intuitive, time-tested strategies rooted in body intelligence. And now, science is catching up. We know that calmness before a meal primes the body for better digestion, absorption, and even portion control.

Rooted in ancient Indian traditions, the timeless wisdom of a pre-meal pause has guided generations toward mindful eating. In India, a silent prayer before eating isn't only about reverence—it's a pause to ground yourself, express gratitude and send a clear signal to your body: it's time to receive.

In Japan, saying *itadakimasu* isn't rushed or robotic—it's a respectful acknowledgement of the food and those who prepared it. A breath of intention before a single bite.

In traditional Chinese medicine, calming the mind before eating is just as vital as the meal itself. A scattered mind, they say, scatters digestion.

These rituals were never just about tradition. They were—and still are—biological cues. Gentle, powerful ways of telling the body: now is the time to nourish, not just consume; now is the time to slow down, not speed through.

They remind us of something modern life too often overlooks: digestion doesn't begin in the mouth. It begins in the mind.

When Ancient Wisdom Meets Modern Gut Health: The Link between Pausing and Digestion

- Ayurveda teaches that Agni—the digestive fire—thrives in a calm, centred state. A mindful pause before meals is essential to awaken it.
- Ancient Greek medicine emphasized eating in a relaxed state—Hippocrates believed digestion worked best when the nervous system was calm.
- Traditional Chinese medicine links digestion directly to emotional balance, with emphasis on stillness before meals.
- In Native American traditions, a quiet moment of reflection honours the meal. In Japan, itadakimasu signals readiness and gratitude.

Together, these ancient teachings reveal a universal truth: When we invite calm and intention before eating, we don't just prepare food—we prepare the whole body to nourish, heal and thrive.

The Eighty Per Cent Rule: Your Stomach's Best Friend

Here's one of the simplest, most effective digestion hacks: Stop eating when you're about eighty per cent full. Not stuffed—just satisfied. Your stomach isn't a storage bin—it's a finely tuned system designed to signal when it's had enough.

This idea isn't new. The Japanese call it Hara Hachi Bu,

a practice tied to longevity. Ayurveda teaches moderation to protect your digestive fire. Modern science backs it up, showing portion control helps metabolism and keeps weight in check.

Put this together with the 7 Breaths Practice, and something shifts—you stop eating because you feel content, guided by calm and awareness, not because there's no food left on your plate.

Real-World Results

When I first introduced this simple breathing practice in a busy corporate environment, I wasn't sure what to expect. But the responses were quick and eye-opening:

- Rahul, a finance manager, said, 'I never realized how much I was overeating just because I was rushing.'
- Maya from marketing shared, 'The bloating I used to live with? Gone. All I did was the 7 Breaths Practice.'
- And a month later, Amit, a senior VP, messaged me: 'No diet, no drama. I've lost three kilos.'

It's proof that sometimes the simplest shifts—like pausing to breathe—can make the biggest difference.

Myth vs Fact

Myth: 7 Breaths to Slimming is a diet.

Fact: It's a simple practice—a pause to breathe before you eat.

Myth: You need to overhaul your meals.

Fact: Just change how much you eat—not what you eat—

guided by your body's signals, which become clearer with conscious breathing.

Myth: It takes weeks to feel a difference.

Fact: You'll feel lighter from your very first meal.

NamitaSpeaks

Pause before you plate. Digestion doesn't start with food—it starts with readiness, initiated by your breath. The 7 Breaths to Slimming is your gentle reset. So, pause. Breathe. Then eat. Your gut will thank you. Your energy will rise. And your waistline? It too may just thank you—quietly but clearly.

2

Pre-Meal Pause: Beat the Post-Meal Slump

Let's begin with something beautifully simple—so simple, in fact, that it often slips by unnoticed. It's that quiet moment just before a meal—whether it's a rushed snack between meetings or a slow, indulgent Sunday brunch. That brief pause when your food is in front of you, but you haven't taken your first bite yet. That pause? It's pure gold. It holds quiet power—a chance to consciously reset.

Because in that tiny moment, you have a powerful choice: eat with awareness—or dive in mindlessly, like a sleep-deprived college student devouring instant noodles at midnight.

This is where a small yet transformative practice comes in—so subtle that it slips into your routine without fanfare. It's called 7 Breaths to Slimming. This gentle practice helps build a healthier relationship with food, encourages better portion control and reduces stress-driven overeating. Over time, it can guide you steadily towards your weight goals.

Before you roll your eyes and think 'not another self-help or diet thing,' let's clear that up right now. This isn't a diet. It's not about counting calories, cutting carbs or feeling guilty for loving food. And it's definitely not your typical self-help spiel. The intention here is not to be preachy, but to promote a mindful eating practice.

It's a practice—a simple yet powerful way to use your breath to support natural, intuitive eating. With just seven slimming breaths, you can reset your system, tune in to your body's cues and refocus. It's about reclaiming control—over how you eat, why you eat, and how much.

One simple practice. Seven breaths. Before every meal. A pause of under two minutes—to breathe, reset and ground yourself before the first bite. Simple. Subtle. Surprisingly effective.

Curious to know more?

The Power of the Pause

The idea is almost suspiciously simple—so simple your brain might dismiss it as ineffective. But don't be fooled. Just pause before eating. Take seven deep, intentional breaths, keeping your breath steady. That's it.

And that tiny pause? It can shift everything. No complicated rituals. No chewing-tracker apps. No smart fork buzzing at you through Bluetooth.

Just you and your breath—your quiet, constant companion, finally stepping into the spotlight.

These 7 Breaths act like a speed bump on the fast, chaotic highway of impulsive eating—helping you slow down, tune in and eat with intention.

The Pause That Changes Everything

You know those moments when your stomach growls and your brain short-circuits? One second, you're lunging at your food like it's an emergency. Then—you pause. You inhale. Exhale. You notice.

And in that pause, something small but profound shifts.

You go from 'I need this NOW or I'll implode' to 'Wait... do I even want all of this?'

From 'Rough day. I deserve this cake,' to 'Rough day. I'll enjoy this cake—but I won't inhale it.'

It's not about being perfect or righteous at the dinner table. It's about presence. Choosing, not reacting. Responding, not just consuming.

Because in that pause you're not just catching your breath—you're catching yourself.

And sometimes that's everything. It shows how this simple pause leads to a brief moment of introspection that not only helps you make better decisions but also holds your hand towards mindful eating.

The Wedding Buffet Test

Imagine the day—you're at a grand Indian wedding—the kind with more guests than a small town and fairy lights brighter than Diwali. The air is thick with spices and sugar. The buffet stretches into infinity—shimmering biryani, decadent butter paneer, golden-fried starters and a dessert counter that looks like heaven's sweet shop.

Your stomach growls. Your brain short-circuits. A voice whispers, 'We came for the bride, but we're leaving with a serious food coma.' The food is winning.

Then—a small act of quiet rebellion. You pause. Step slightly away from the crowd, close your eyes for a moment or simply look up for a second of buffet clarity. And breathe. One breath…then another. Seven in total.

No, it's not just another fleeting wellness craze. It's presence.

You open your eyes. The buffet's still there, still tempting. But you've shifted. A quiet moment of realization happens. You move calmly. Choose consciously. Take what you truly want—not what the crowd or social pressure nudges you towards.

You eat. You savour. And you stop—before regret sets in.

Here's the twist: You didn't restrict yourself. You didn't do mental math about detoxing tomorrow. You didn't demonize the gulab jamun (because really, it's just doing its job).

You simply remembered: You're the one holding the plate. Seven breaths stood between you and mindless overeating.

In that pause, real transformation begins—right in that simple moment of choice.

Why Good Intentions Fail (Hint: It's Not You)

Let's be real. You start the day strong—smoothie in hand, veggies packed, infused water bottle by your side. Then mid-afternoon hits. You're tired. Stressed. Someone mentions burgers and fries...and suddenly you're elbow-deep in snacks you didn't want, need or even enjoy.

It's not about willpower. It's not a moral failing. You just missed the moment before.

That fleeting pause where intention could've turned into action. That's exactly where 7 Breaths to Slimming steps in.

It's that crucial pause before eating—where intention finally has a chance to become a conscious choice. And that's what makes this practice a quiet game-changer.

It doesn't shout. It doesn't judge. It simply inserts awareness into that tiny sliver of time...creating space for real change to begin.

Not Just Weddings: The Many Faces of Mindless Eating

You don't need a wedding buffet to lose control around food. Mindless eating shows up everywhere:

- In the car, stressed and grabbing snacks between errands.
- At your desk, eating lunch while juggling forty-seven unread emails.
- On the couch, where meals become background noise to your latest Netflix binge.
- During holidays, when every meal feels like a free-for-all.
- At family gatherings, where 'no, thanks' feels like an insult.
- While travelling, when routine disappears and eating turns into survival mode.
- At those unlimited breakfast buffets that come free with your hotel stay.
- Even at the grocery store, munching through the aisles without noticing.

What's the common thread? No pause. No breath. Just a blur of bites and emotions.

The good news? The 7 Breaths Practice can gently break the cycle. Pause. Breathe. Choose. Take back control—one meal, one breath at a time.

Meera's Garlic Bread Redemption

Let me tell you about Meera, a college friend of mine and a classic carb-avoider. One evening at a dinner party, she faced her two greatest temptations: good friends and irresistible garlic bread.

She showed up determined—'No bread tonight,' she said firmly. Ten minutes later? Two slices down, muttering, 'I'll skip dessert to make up for it.'

(Spoiler alert: She didn't skip dessert. She added a slice

of cake on top. Then felt guilty. Then ate more to feel better. Sound familiar?)

The next time, Meera tried something radical—at least by dinner party standards. Before reaching for her plate, she paused. Closed her eyes—not in prayer, but in presence.

Then she took seven slow, deliberate breaths, focusing only on her breathing. She grounded herself in the moment, letting the garlic bread urge rise…and pass.

Did she still eat the garlic bread? Yes—but just one glorious, golden slice. Did she enjoy dessert? Absolutely—but just a few bites, not a full-on sugar spiral.

When Meera left that dinner, something had shifted. She wasn't bloated. She wasn't guilty. And she wasn't spiralling into 'I'll start over tomorrow' mode.

She felt proud. Grounded. In control.

That pause didn't steal her pleasure. It didn't ask her to resist joy. It simply reminded her of one quiet truth: food doesn't make the rules; you do.

Later that week, she found herself reaching for a snack purely out of habit—not hunger.

Her hand hovered over the cupboard, and she paused, just like she had at the dinner.

Seven slow breaths.

In that tiny moment of presence, she realized she didn't actually want the snack.

What she truly needed was a break, a breath, a reset.

The Science behind the Pause

Does pausing before a meal really make a difference? If all this talk about breathing and slowing down feels like a Zen retreat crashing your dinner party—don't worry. It's grounded in well-established science. Here's the simple version.

Taking a few slow, deep breaths before eating activates your parasympathetic nervous system—your body's 'rest and digest' mode. It sends a calming message to your system: 'We're safe. It's okay to slow down.' In this relaxed state, stress hormones like cortisol begin to drop. That matters, because elevated cortisol can increase cravings and contribute to belly fat. Why is this important? Because when your body is calm, it's more efficient at absorbing nutrients instead of hoarding calories like it's preparing for a famine.

There's more: deep breathing activates your prefrontal cortex—the part of your brain responsible for decision-making, impulse control and staying aligned with your goals. So, before you reach for that third chocolate chip cookie or fried samosa, your brain gets a moment to ask: 'Do I really want this?' This isn't a breathing performance—it's a practice that shifts you from reactivity to awareness.

Did you know? Distracted eating can increase food intake by up to twenty-five per cent. That's not just a few extra bites—it's nearly a quarter of a meal your body didn't ask for. While your brain was multitasking, your fork just kept going.

And when it comes to stress? Deep breathing helps lower cortisol, the hormone that spikes under pressure. Chronically high cortisol is linked to sugar cravings, belly fat and that irresistible urge to snack even when you're full.

Dr Elissa Epel, a leading researcher on stress and eating behaviours, notes: 'Simple breathing exercises engage the body's relaxation response, which can reduce stress-related overeating and support healthier eating choices.'

Her findings, described extensively in *The Telomere Effect* (co-authored with Nobel laureate Elizabeth Blackburn) and in her research on stress physiology, reinforce how a brief pause—especially through breathwork—can shift the body into a calmer, more mindful state before eating.[1]

So, no—it's not woo-woo. It's science. Backed by your breath.

Anchoring the Habit in Real Life

Let's be real—good intentions often get lost in the chaos of daily life. Deadlines, distractions and stress can easily push healthy habits aside. That's why your pause needs simple reminders—anchors to bring you back. Try these:

- A sticky note on your fridge or lunchbox: 'Pause. Breathe. Then eat.'
- A gentle phone alarm at mealtimes.
- A calming screensaver or wallpaper.
- Or get playful—stick a Post-it on your plate that says, 'Breathe, darling.'

Before you know it, you'll catch yourself mid-action, hand hovering over that extra bite. And that moment of awareness? That's the real win.

This is bigger than food. This practice isn't just about what you eat—it's about how you show up for yourself every day. Each breath is a small but powerful way to say: 'I'm here. I'm intentional. I respect my body.'

By starting every meal with seven breaths, you build

---

[1]Blackburn, Elizabeth H., and Elissa Epel, *The Telomere Effect: A Revolutionary Approach to Living Younger, Healthier, Longer*, Grand Central Publishing, New York, 2017.

self-trust and gain control—not through restriction, but through presence. Let your hunger meet clarity instead of chaos.

Beyond food, this simple habit can help you feel more grounded and lower stress throughout your day. It's about creating space to live with calm, purpose and kindness towards yourself.

NamitaSpeaks

Pausing isn't a delay—it's a decision. A decision to eat with intention. To live with awareness. To take 7 Breaths before your first bite. Try it today—see how it feels. Pause. Breathe. Begin. Bon appétit.

3

The Diet Reset

No more chasing someone else's perfect plan. Let your breath lead the way back to you.

Bio-individuality: Why One Diet Doesn't Fit All

Ever wonder why your friend drops two kilos without even trying, while you survive on kale and air and the scale won't budge? We've all seen it: two people follow the same trendy diet—keto, vegan, or 'I-only-eat-air-before-noon'—and one is glowing and shrinking, while the other feels bloated, miserable and questioning all their life choices. The answer lies in the powerful concept of **bio-individuality**.

It's a fancy term for a simple truth: your body isn't a clone of someone else's. It's not just about willpower—it's about biology and lifestyle. Your activity levels, metabolism, gut bacteria, hormone balance, stress responses, genes and even your emotional relationship with food are uniquely yours.

So, when you copy someone's miracle diet and expect the same results, it's like trying to run a high-tech app on outdated software—it simply doesn't work with your system. Own your fit.

The Diet Carousel: Confusion and Cravings

Just when you've stocked up on almond butter and coconut flakes, a new study declares carbs are back. Or out. Or completely off the map. Fats were once evil—now they're sacred. Six small meals? Nope—fast for sixteen hours and eat within a two-hour window. If trends keep flipping the way they are, next week's superfood might just be water blessed by moonlight!

If you're not confused by modern nutrition advice, are you even paying attention?

Here's the refreshing fact: **you are the best nutritionist you'll ever have**. Your body already knows what works—you just need to stop drowning in the noise long enough to listen.

7 Breaths to Slimming: Your Universal Reset Button

In a whirlwind of diet fads and confusing food rules, there's one simple practice that goes well with every approach—whether you're into naturopathy, an ayurvedic lifestyle, a keto or a gluten-free diet, veganism, intermittent fasting, or just savouring your grandma's comforting rajma-chawal.

Meet 7 Breaths to Slimming: a quick, powerful reset for your body and mind that cuts through the noise and helps you tune in to what truly works for you. This isn't about *what* you eat—it's about *how* much you eat, and *how* fully present you are while eating. No matter your eating style, 7 Breaths to Slimming offers a universal reset that fits seamlessly with any diet plan. Before every meal, pause. Take seven deep, intentional breaths. Then begin to eat.

By increasing your body awareness and easing stress-driven

cravings through breathing, this simple practice can quietly support your journey toward your weight goals—regardless of the cuisine or nutrition plan.

That's the beauty of it—simple yet powerful. You grow more in tune with your hunger cues, better at managing portions and more likely to truly enjoy your meals. As you take these breaths, tune in to the sensations in your body. Does slowing your breath bring a calmness that stays with you as you start eating? This small pause holds the potential to transform your relationship with food—one breath at a time.

How the 7 Breaths Practice Supports Different Diets

Let's discover how this simple breath practice can effortlessly complement any diet you follow. The 7 Breaths Practice supports each eating style in its own unique way. Here's how it can help you, whatever your plate looks like:

Keto Diet

High-fat, low-carb meals are designed to trigger ketosis.

Why the breath practice helps: Keto meals can be rich and filling—sometimes even too much so. This practice helps you recognize when you're truly satisfied, preventing overeating.

Intermittent Fasting

An eating pattern that cycles between periods of fasting and eating, such as:

- 16:8: Fast for sixteen hours and eat within an eight-hour window.

- OMAD (One Meal A Day): Fast for around twenty-three hours and eat one main meal a day.

Why the breath practice helps: After prolonged fasting, hunger can feel intense, often leading to rushed or excessive eating. Taking these breaths creates an intentional pause, helping you move from reactive hunger to nourishment.

Plant-Based/Vegan Diet

Centred around vegetables, fruits, legumes, whole grains, nuts and seeds.

Why the breath practice helps: Plant-based meals are wholesome but can be easy to overconsume. This practice reconnects you to your body's signals, so you eat what you need—not just everything in front of you.

Ayurvedic Diet (Sattvic Eating)

Based on balancing your dosha (body type)—vata (air/space), pitta (fire/water) or kapha (earth/water).

Why the breath practice helps: Ayurveda emphasizes calm eating. The breath practice aligns beautifully with this philosophy, grounding your energy and helping you eat in harmony with your body's needs.

Mediterranean Diet

Rich in olive oil, legumes, vegetables, fruits, dairy and whole grains.

Why the breath practice helps: These meals are delicious and satisfying, but it's easy to overdo it. The breath practice helps you enjoy every bite and stop when you're full—not stuffed.

Traditional Asian Diets

Emphasizing rice or noodles, vegetables, tofu, seaweed and fermented foods.

Why the breath practice helps: Many Asian cultures treat meals as a sacred experience. This practice deepens that awareness, adding intention to your eating and encouraging portion control.

Calorie Counting/Structured Eating

Tracking intake through apps or pre-planned meals.

Why the breath practice helps: With all the calorie math, eating can feel robotic. The breath practice shifts you from numbers to nourishment—from tracking to tuning in.

No Formal Diet

Whether you're eating home-cooked meals, dining out or simply going by hunger.

Why the breath practice helps: Without rules or structure, it's easy to eat on autopilot. The breath practice becomes your anchor, helping you shift from reactive to responsive eating.

In essence, 7 Breaths to Slimming serves as your built-in pause button—a gentle reset, a moment of calm and a return to awareness, no matter what you eat.

The Dreaded Diet Plateau: When Progress Hits Pause

Every diet begins with a burst of enthusiasm—you feel lighter, energized and hopeful. A few kilos drop and you wonder, 'Why didn't I start sooner?' Then suddenly, the scale stalls. Your body adapts, motivation fades and life gets hectic. Missed meals turn into binges. Before long, the weight creeps back, and you find yourself saying, 'Monday, I'll start again.'

Here's the truth: this is exactly when 7 Breaths to Slimming becomes your ultimate reset button.

This simple breath practice grounds you in the moment and reconnects you to your weight goals. Even when your diet derails, these breaths help steady your focus and support your slimming journey.

Real People, Real Aha! Moments

Many people first heard about the 7 Breaths to Slimming through my talks, consultations or wellness workshops. What they discovered was surprising—this simple breath practice wasn't just a pause. It could become a turning point.

Priya, the Keto Enthusiast: She started strong on a high-fat, low-carb plan but soon felt sluggish and bloated.

Enter 7 Breaths: The breath practice helped her tune in to how foods made her feel and notice when she was truly full.

'I stopped eating just because it fit the plan. The breath helped me notice what my body actually needed.'

Rahul, the Intermittent Faster: He fasted with discipline but broke it like a race to the finish line.

Enter 7 Breaths: Intentional breaths before eating helped him slow down and avoid the all-or-nothing trap.

'I stopped eating like I was starving. This helped me find my rhythm.'

Amrita, the Ayurveda Follower: She stuck to sattvic foods, but her meals were rushed—in the car, between meetings, during Zoom calls.

Enter 7 Breaths: With just a short pause, she shifted from chaos to calm, bringing presence to every meal.

'The food didn't change. I did. These breaths helped me eat with attention.'

Sameer, the Balanced Eater (except after 9 p.m.): His days were clean and structured, but the nights brought endless snacking.

Enter 7 Breaths: Before reaching for something, he'd take a few breaths—often enough to regain clarity and choose differently.

'I didn't change what I ate. I changed how and how much I ate. The breath gave me back control.'

Each of them experienced what so many others have found: **7 Breaths to Slimming works**. Because it creates a moment of clarity, calm and control in the most important place of all—between the urge and the action.

Your Body Is Talking to You. Are You Listening?

After every meal, check in with yourself:

- Do I feel light or weighed down?
- Am I energized or fatigued?
- Am I truly satisfied or still craving more?

Your body offers constant feedback. That's your real guide—not someone else's rules about what you should eat.

Diet Myths That Need a Reality Check

Myth: It's gluten-free, so I can eat the whole pack.
Fact: Gluten-free doesn't mean calorie-free. Moderation still matters.
Myth: It's within my eating window; I can go overboard.
Fact: Time doesn't justify overeating. Quantity still counts.
Myth: Low-fat means I can eat more.
Fact: Low-fat often means high sugar. Eating more can lead to weight gain. Read the labels—don't be misled.

7 Breaths to Slimming: A Reset for Your Journey

This breath practice is your tool to break the cycle of reactive, guilt-driven eating.

- It helps you pause, reset and choose with awareness.
- Your diet doesn't define you—your awareness does.
- There's no one-size-fits-all approach to eating.

This isn't about restriction—it's about reconnection. With your body. Your rhythm. Your inner wisdom.

Can't do seven full breaths yet? Start with three. Make them subtle if you're out in public. The key is simply to pause. Create a moment that works for you.

NamitaSpeaks

Before you eat, pause and take 7 Breaths.
Let your breath lead the way—your body will follow.
This isn't about control—it's about connection.

4

Global Foods, Slimming Secrets

Eat Global, Stay Slim: Ever wonder how people worldwide enjoy rich, flavourful foods and still stay slim and healthy?

What if I told you the secret isn't just in what they eat, but how they eat?

Whether you're a student abroad, a globe-trotting CEO or someone who loves travel and cuisines from around the world, mastering the art of portion control lets you savour your cravings without derailing your slimming goals.

The other day, I found myself in a delightfully artisanal chocolate boutique in Mumbai (because honestly, who doesn't want to go a little gourmet while giving in to a sugar craving?). But what caught my attention wasn't just the luxurious treats, the cocoa percentage or the gold-dusted truffles—it was the size of these chocolates. Each piece was tiny, almost dainty, designed not to overwhelm but to delight. It was mindful indulgence at its finest—a clever psychology that worked. The goal wasn't to deny the craving but to embrace it with awareness. Sometimes, the real treat is knowing when to stop.

And you know what? It worked. It wasn't about fighting the cravings, it was about meeting them halfway, with a bit of awareness and a pinch of restraint. A clever psychological masterstroke wrapped in shiny paper.

Sometimes, the real treat isn't finishing the whole bar—it's realizing you're perfectly content after just one piece. (Well… maybe two. Let's not pretend we're superhuman!)

A friend's daughter recently returned from Paris and laughed when she described how her host family would slice a small piece of Camembert cheese and make it last three bites, while discussing philosophy at the table. 'It's like they were tasting time itself,' she said. No rush. Just presence. It reminded her that food isn't always about quantity—it's about connection. No rush. No mindless grazing. Just presence.

After all, the slimming journey can't sustain itself on rigid restrictions. It's about understanding that sometimes just a little is more than enough. So, as you explore the diverse culinary world, remember:

You don't have to give up your favourite foods—it's about how you enjoy them, not just how much.

Cultural Cues to Conscious Eating

Now, let's take a culinary tour around the world. Picture this: you're wandering through Tokyo's buzzing food stalls, or sipping coffee on a sunny terrace in Barcelona, or sharing a meal in a tranquil Balinese home. Each culture brings its culinary treasures—and its wisdom about how to eat. What can we learn from them?

I once asked a Japanese exchange student how she managed to stay so effortlessly energetic, even though she ate rice and noodles every day. She smiled and said, 'I listen to my stomach, not my plate.' That simple phrase stayed with me.

How often do we finish everything on our plates, not because we're hungry, but because it's there?

From Japan's Hara Hachi Bu—stop eating when you're eighty per cent full—to France's *Joie de Manger*, the joy of savouring each bite, and Bali's *Tri Hita Karana*, which emphasizes balance between humans, nature and gratitude—even at the table, these practices remind us that eating is about listening to our body's true needs. Even in the world of business, many seasoned dealmakers avoid eating until they're full, believing a heavy stomach clouds the mind and dulls judgement, inhibiting sharp decision-making. They prefer negotiating on a lighter, clearer stomach, showing that the idea of stopping before fullness lives not just in ancient philosophies, but in practical, even material, wisdom.

The Wisdom behind Global Eating Habits

Across these cultures, the central idea is the same: Food is more than fuel; it's an experience. One to be respected, savoured and enjoyed with control.

Let's break down the key principles:

- **France:** How do the French enjoy creamy, full-fat cheese and still stay slim? They savour small portions, eat slowly and stop when satisfied, turning each bite into an experience.
- **Japan:** How do the Japanese live long, healthy lives while enjoying rice and noodles? They practise Hara Hachi Bu—eating until they're only eighty per cent full, guided by mindful awareness of hunger cues.
- **Italy:** How do Italians indulge in pasta without weight gain? They prioritize quality over quantity, eat slowly and enjoy their meals without distraction.

- **Okinawa:** How do Okinawans stay lean and vibrant into old age? They eat a variety of fresh vegetables and fish in modest portions, a practice rooted in the principle of moderation.

Notice the Pattern?

Across continents and cuisines, one universal truth stands out: Staying healthy isn't about restriction or deprivation—it's about intention. The flavours may change from country to country, but the focus remains the same: portion control and respecting your body's needs. Staying slim isn't about rules, it's about aligning your habits with your goals in a consistent, conscious way.

But Here's the Key

No tradition, however wise, can guide you unless you choose to live it. I once witnessed this choice in action. At a wellness retreat in Bali, I noticed a woman pause before every meal—eyes closed, breathing slowly. Curious, I asked her about it.

'*It's my way of saying thank you to the food,*' she said. '*It's a reminder to eat with kindness, not urgency.*'

It was beautiful in its simplicity—an intentional pause that turned an ordinary meal into a quiet ritual.

The Power of Seven Breaths

Before your next meal—whether it's a Gujarati thali in India, sushi in Tokyo or an avocado bowl in California—pause. Take seven slow, conscious breaths. This simple yet powerful practice brings you into the present moment.

It helps you tune in to your hunger cues and stop when you're full. In those breaths, the mental chatter softens and your body's signals become clearer—an essential step towards eating in tune with your true needs.

Make It Your Own

Try this the next time you sit down to eat:

- Take a deep breath.
- As you inhale, tune in to your body's needs.
- As you exhale, let go of any stress or urgency.
- Now, imagine taking in seven breaths before a meal.

That's what this book is about—creating a pause, a moment of awareness.

With practice, you'll feel more in tune with your body and more in control of your choices.

You can also try a few slow breaths when a craving arises—it might help you check if it's true hunger or something else.

These breaths help you slow down, tune in, eat the right amount and feel satisfied, not stuffed. It's a simple, timeless way to bring awareness to every meal.

Superpower Breathing: Real Stories and Inspirations

A friend who's a busy mom recently told me how she introduced my 'seven breaths' practice to her young children as a fun mealtime ritual.

'They call it "Superpower Breathing" now,' she smiled, *'and it's helped them slow down and eat in a relaxed manner.'*

At a wellness retreat in Kerala, I met a corporate executive who shared how discovering the power of those slow breaths before meals—my practice—gave her a much-needed moment of calm during hectic days and helped her avoid stress eating.

The idea of *lagom*, a Swedish word meaning 'just enough', perfectly echoes the principles behind my seven breaths practice. I first read about this concept in a book on Scandinavian lifestyle and nutrition, and it reinforced the importance of finding balance and eating in tune with what feels right. In Sweden, lagom isn't just a word—it's a way of life. It guides everyday choices, from modest portion sizes to unhurried meals, reflecting a cultural value of balance and moderation.

Words to Eat by: The World's Wisdom on Your Plate

Here are some timeless phrases from cultures around the world—simple expressions carrying centuries of wisdom that guide us toward healthier eating:

- **Hara Hachi Bu** *(Japan)*—Eat until you're eighty per cent full
- **Lagom** *(Sweden)*—Just enough; the sweet spot between too little and too much
- **Joie de Manger***(France)*—The joy of eating with pleasure and presence
- **La Dolce Vita** *(Italy)*—The sweet life: eat slowly, joyfully and socially
- **Tri Hita Karana** *(Bali)*—Harmony between self, others, and nature—even at the table
- **Oryoki** *(Zen Buddhism)*—Eat with quiet gratitude, taking only what is needed
- **Bapsang** *(Korea)*—A balanced, beautiful spread that nourishes the whole being

- **Sattvic** *(India)*—Eating clean, calming foods to nourish both body and mind

Flavours may change, but the essence of intentional eating remains constant—presence, balance and joy. These aren't just catchy phrases; they are guiding principles for living a healthier, more balanced life.

Embrace them not as rules, but as invitations to savour your eating experience while still aligning with your slimming goals.

NamitaSpeaks

Food is a global experience—from the vibrant flavours of tacos in Mexico to the rich spices of Indian curries. Weight loss isn't about restrictions; it's about rhythm and balance. 7 Breaths to Slimming is simple yet powerful—and can be done anywhere.

No diets. No guilt. Just pause, breathe and eat with intention. Because ultimately, it's not about what's on your plate—it's about how you show up to eat it.

5

Mastery through Breath: How 7 Breaths Can Transform Your Eating Habits

Is discipline something you're born with, or something you build?

Discipline isn't about restriction—it's about control. And control starts with a calm mind.

James Clear, bestselling author of *Atomic Habits*, shows us something profound: small, consistent actions can rebuild an entire life. After a devastating baseball accident in his teenage years, James was left with injuries so severe that even basic tasks felt overwhelming. But here's the thing—he didn't claw his way back through grand gestures or heroic resolutions. He started tiny: stretching for just a few minutes, lifting the lightest weights, writing a single sentence. Day by day, these small, almost invisible habits stacked up.[2]

Over time, they built the foundation for the disciplined, high-performing life he leads today. From the outside, it might look like James was born with natural talent. In reality, what we're seeing is years of patient, steady habit-building. And that

[2]Clear, James, *Atomic Habits: An Easy & Proven Way to Build Good Habits & Break Bad Ones*, Avery, New York, 2018.

brings us to a truth we don't talk about enough: discipline isn't just a trait you're born with. Discipline is a skill—a talent you develop over time.

Building Discipline One Step at a Time

Yes, it's hard at first. Yes, most people struggle. Research even shows that it typically takes at least twenty-one days—and often longer—for a new habit to truly take root. Forming discipline is like building a muscle: awkward and frustrating in the beginning, but once strengthened, it becomes a part of who you are. It doesn't just help you achieve big goals; it supports the small, daily choices that lead to lasting change.

When it comes to weight loss or simply healthier living, it's usually not the 'big meals' that sabotage progress. It's the lack of awareness around the small things: mindless nibbling, stress eating, emotional snacking. Most people don't struggle with what they eat at mealtimes; they struggle with cravings, with impulse decisions made in fleeting moments. And that's exactly where many good intentions fall apart. You don't gain weight because you lack knowledge. You struggle because your day is filled with tiny, unconscious choices that add up.

Cravings and Emotions

Cravings often have little to do with real, physical hunger and have everything to do with your emotional state. When stress or anxiety kicks in, it hijacks the part of your brain responsible for thoughtful decision-making. In those moments, it's not that you lack discipline. Your body is simply doing what it's wired to do: chasing quick comfort, trying to self-soothe in the fastest, most familiar way it knows how, often through food. At the time of stress, before reaching for food, try taking a few slow, conscious breaths. Notice if it creates a small space, a moment to choose a different response.

But imagine this: What if you didn't have to fight harder to stay in control? What if you didn't have to wrestle with yourself at all? What if the answer wasn't some big, dramatic solution, but something simple and quietly powerful? That's the shift. Instead of reacting impulsively, you pause. Instead of chasing quick fixes, you breathe. That's the promise of 7 Breaths to Slimming. It's not about forcing yourself into rigid control. It's about creating calmness, the space where better decisions naturally happen.

It helps you move from mindless reaction to mindful intention, not by pushing harder, but by stepping into awareness, one breath at a time. And like any meaningful change, it's not a one-time trick—it's a habit you build, a discipline you nurture, day after day. The more you practise it, the more natural it becomes—until it's no longer something you have to remember, but simply a part of who you are. Small acts, practised consistently, create extraordinary change. 7 Breaths to Slimming could be the beginning of a lifetime of calm, quiet strength.

7 Breaths to Slimming: Your Superpower

This isn't just any breathing technique—it's an intentional pause. Not the kind where you debate whether to eat one cookie…or three. This is a focused, deliberate moment designed to create a powerful shift.

Just seven slow, conscious breaths before a meal can work wonders, like shifting from chaos into calm. This simple practice acts as a bridge between stress and stillness, transforming eating from a mindless reflex into a mindful choice.

By regularly connecting with your breath, you heighten your awareness of your body's true hunger and fullness cues, as well as the subtle shifts in your emotional state. This interoceptive awareness becomes your secret weapon, helping you make more conscious, disciplined choices aligned with your well-being.

And remember: the best way to breathe is the way that feels natural and calming for you. If seven breaths feel like too much, start with three. It's the intention behind the pause—and the act of tuning in—that truly makes the difference.

7 Breaths to Slimming isn't a diet—it's a daily discipline. A chance to reset, slow down and reconnect with your body's natural intelligence before each meal. The slimming effect doesn't come from restriction, but from self-awareness. This leads to healthier habits, more balanced portions and a more intentional approach to nourishment.

Why Stress Weakens Discipline

Ever wonder why your best intentions seem to vanish the moment stress shows up? It's not just bad luck—it's biology. When you're under stress, your body shifts into survival mode, making it harder to stick to thoughtful choices and long-term goals.

Here's what's happening behind the scenes:

- Your brain shifts into high-alert mode.
- Your body craves quick, comforting rewards (often unhealthy ones).
- Your decisions become reactive instead of intentional.

Understanding this isn't about blaming yourself—it's about recognizing how your system works, so you can start working with it, not against it. No wonder it's hard to stop at just one slice of pizza or a single doughnut—your nervous system is simply doing what it was designed to do.

7 Breaths to Calm and Control

With each deliberate breath, your brain receives a calming message: 'You're safe. No need to rush or react.'

This rhythm engages your body's relaxation response, gently easing you out of stress and into calm. The benefits include:

- Reducing levels of cortisol, the stress hormone
- Sharpening mental clarity and focus
- Building a moment of space between impulse and action

By tuning in to the subtle rise and fall of your breath—the coolness as air enters, the warmth as it leaves—you deepen your connection to the present moment. This increased body awareness empowers you to notice urges without immediately acting on them.

In that brief pause, you regain control. You choose your response, rather than giving in to automatic cravings.

Real-Life Case Studies: Small Changes, Big Impact

It's easy to assume that lasting transformation requires big, dramatic shifts. But often, it's the smallest habits that make the biggest difference. These real-life stories show how simple changes, like the 7 Breaths Practice, can lead to lasting wellness and powerful results. Here's how a few everyday people turned a simple pause into meaningful change.

1. **The Corporate Hustler:** Thomas, a senior tech executive, was the classic multitasker—grabbing bites between back-to-back Zoom calls, barely noticing what he was eating. Diets, detoxes, fasting—you name it, he had tried it. Nothing seemed to stick. Then he heard about the 7 Breaths Practice during a wellness webinar he attended out of curiosity and thought. 'It's just breathing—why not give it a chance?' 'At first, it sounded way too simple to work,' Thomas admitted. 'But those seven breaths slowed me down. My cravings eased up. I lost two kilos in one month—without changing what I ate, just how I approached my meals.' Today, '7 Breaths' lunches have become a quiet wellness ritual within his entire office team—a reminder that presence at the table pays off far beyond the plate.
2. **The Busy Homemaker:** Sunita, a mother of two, often found herself mindlessly finishing her kids' leftovers—not because she was hungry, but simply out of habit. She wasn't eating consciously; she was operating on autopilot. She first heard about the 7 Breaths Practice at a friend's house over coffee, and it struck a chord. 'Now I pause and take seven breaths,' she says. 'That pause makes me ask—am I hungry, or just tired?' That tiny shift in awareness helped Sunita lose three kilos in just two months, without restrictive diets—simply by tuning in to her body's true needs.
3. **The Tennis Enthusiast:** Amit, a passionate tennis

player, struggled with overeating on his high-intensity training days. Fuelling himself for performance often blurred into emotional eating. He learned about the 7 Breaths Practice after attending a sports nutrition workshop where the idea of disciplined eating was discussed. Once he incorporated the practice before his meals, everything started to change. 'The seven breaths help me eat with purpose,' Amit shares. 'When I feel centred, I fuel—I don't binge. I feel lighter and more energetic now. I carry that focus into the court as well. It's not just about eating better; it's about playing stronger.'

An Experiment You Can Try Today

Next time you reach for a snack or sit down for a meal, experiment with one breath. Pause. Take a deep breath. Relax. Then ask yourself, 'Am I truly hungry, or am I just eating out of habit—or to satisfy an emotion?' It's a small act, but it can shift your entire mindset. Extend this experiment beyond meals. When you feel a craving arise, pause and take just one conscious breath. Observe what happens. This simple experiment with one breath can change how you approach food. Now, imagine the power of seven breaths—this is exactly what the book teaches you. It's where awareness begins, and true transformation follows.

Breathwork behind Mastery

The 7 Breaths to Slimming draws on the same core principles practised by high performers across fields:

- Musicians, who harness breath to steady rhythm and express emotion.
- Elite athletes, who control their breathing to stay focused and composed under pressure.
- Business leaders, who take a moment to centre themselves before critical decisions and high-stakes meetings.

What ties them all together? A simple but powerful pause paired with clear intention.

That's the heart of your 7 Breaths Practice—a purposeful pause that sharpens focus, shifts your state and strengthens self-control, one breath at a time.

NamitaSpeaks

Discipline isn't a diet—it's a mindset. And that mindset starts with just seven conscious breaths. Let 7 Breaths to Slimming be your anchor.

This simple, powerful habit might just be the game-changer your weight-loss journey has been waiting for.

SECTION TWO

7 Breaths to Slimming: How It Works

In today's fast-paced world, breathing is a powerful tool for slimming. This section explores how 7 Breaths to Slimming aligns with weight-loss goals. By shifting from stress and mindless eating to calm awareness, the 7 Breaths and Mini Breath practices help reshape habits and promote self-discipline. Whether addressing emotional eating or improving portion control, breath practice offers a simple, effective approach to achieving your slimming goals.

1

Getting Started: FAQs

Tired of the Weight-Loss Battle? What if the Answer Was Already Inside You?

You've navigated the maze of diets, meticulously counted every calorie and pushed through workouts that felt like punishment. Yet, the lasting results you crave remain elusive. What if the key to finally unlocking your body's natural ability to slim down wasn't another external restriction, but a simple, internal shift?

Welcome to a new way of slimming.

This isn't another crash diet. It's a quiet revolution—one that starts with your breath. Before you jump to the questions, pause with us. Open your mind—and allow this simple practice to reveal its transformative power.

Ready for a Slimming Journey with Just 7 Breaths?

True transformation doesn't happen through willpower alone. It begins with awareness, and awareness starts with breath. In a world obsessed with fast fixes, 7 Breaths to Slimming invites you to slow down, tune in and find a new relationship with food—one breath at a time.

You might have some questions. That's natural. After all, we're conditioned to think that change requires struggle. But sometimes, the simplest shifts are the most powerful.

Let's answer a few questions you might have before we begin.

∾

Awareness is the greatest agent for change

—Eckhart Tolle

(i) What is 7 Breaths to Slimming?

It's a gentle and easy practice. There's no specific pace or rhythm you need to force. Just allow your breath to be slow and easy for each inhale and exhale. The focus is simply on that soft, steady rhythm of your breathing and the quiet, supportive affirmations that help you centre yourself before you eat.

(ii) Is 7 Breaths to Slimming another diet?

Not at all! Think of it as a friendly pause, a conscious breath and just seven of them. This book offers a real shift in how you approach eating. It's more than just a technique; it's a whole new way of thinking. True change starts not with what's on your plate, but with your breath. Forget rigid rules and counting; this is about naturally finding the right portions for you, without any pressure or guilt.

(iii) Why does it work?

It works because it's wonderfully simple, and there's real power in that simplicity. It creates a little space between your initial urge to eat and the action of eating. And the beautiful secret? It gently builds discipline from within, quietly and steadily as you practise. That little pause to breathe brings you right back to what's important—your awareness. You become more in tune with not just your state of mind as you eat, but with how much your body truly needs. It's like gently guiding your relationship with food, sharpening your inner strength, clearing your head and guiding you towards your slimming goals.

(iv) What is the science behind it?

It's fascinating! Research in respected journals like *Appetite* and *The American Journal of Clinical Nutrition* has shown that when people take a moment to breathe deeply, stay present and listen to their body's hunger signals, they tend to naturally eat less and make more aware and supportive food choices. One of their key habits? Portion control. They eat at a relaxed pace, really enjoy each bite and know when to stop, feeling nicely satisfied, not overly full. Breathing before meals activates your parasympathetic nervous system—that's your 'rest-and-digest' mode—which helps lower stress hormones like cortisol that can often trigger overeating.

(v) Why is breath the omnipresent channel?

Isn't it amazing? Your breath is always right there with you—steady, silent and incredibly powerful. When you use it intentionally, it becomes a wonderful ally, helping to calm your mind, grounding your emotions and guiding you to eat with wisdom. Think about people who naturally stay slim; they usually don't rely on the latest fads. They often have one core, sustainable habit: they listen to their body and practise portion control. The 7 Breaths Practice helps you gently reconnect with that inner wisdom, so eating becomes something that flows naturally, not something you have to constantly control.

(vi) Why should I do this method of breathing before meals?

That's the perfect moment! It is like hitting a reset button right before you eat. This simple practice helps you pause and centre yourself before you even begin. It gently interrupts patterns of stress eating, emotional snacking and munching before you even start.

(vii) When to use it?
Make this your little practice before every meal and even before snacks. It's especially helpful when you notice yourself reaching for food on autopilot or when emotions are playing a role in your signs of hunger.

(viii) What does it help with?
It's a fantastic support for portion control, and it helps you learn to recognize that comfortable feeling of being about eighty per cent full. It's about tuning into your body's signals.

(ix) How do I measure eighty per cent fullness?
It's a lovely, intuitive process. As you practise, your body will naturally start to communicate with you more clearly. You'll begin to notice a pleasant sense of satisfaction, without that heavy, overly full feeling. It's about learning to listen to those gentle cues.

(x) Do I need to do this before every meal?
Yes, and you know what? It takes less than one minute, but the positive impact on your mindset and your ability to manage portions can be truly significant. It's a small investment for a big reward in how you feel around food.

(xi) Will I hit a plateau?
It's less likely with this approach. As your body gently adjusts, your natural sense of fullness will also evolve. You'll probably find yourself wanting and eating less, all without feeling like you're missing out.

(xii) Do I stop once I reach my target weight?
Think of reaching your goal as a wonderful milestone, but not the finish line. Maintaining success comes from continuing to nurture that inner awareness. The 7 Breaths Practice becomes a lovely, sustainable habit that supports your ongoing connection with your eating habits.

(xiii) What if I have already said a prayer before meals?
That's beautiful! Think of the 7 Breaths Practice as a gentle pause to prepare yourself, almost like a quiet prelude before your prayer. They can flow together so nicely and enhance your sense of presence before you eat.

(xiv) I love the idea, but doing this before every meal feels overwhelming. Can I ease into it?
Absolutely! This is all about creating a positive and sustainable habit, so there's no need to rush. Let's take it step by step, like building any good habit:

> **Week 1:** Just focus on doing it before one meal each day—maybe the one where you tend to eat a bit more, or without really thinking. For many, that's often dinner.
> **Week 2:** Let's add another meal. Perhaps lunch or breakfast. Just practise that same gentle pause.
> **Week 3:** Now you can include the third meal.
> **Week 4:** You'll likely notice that pausing before every meal and snack feels much more natural—a calm and intuitive part of your routine.

Remember, this isn't about perfection; it's about gently weaving this practice into your life. It will grow with your consistency. Your breath becomes a comforting anchor, naturally leading to lasting, positive changes.

Key pointers

- Takes approximately 1 minute. (7 Breaths ≈ 1 minute)
- Each breath (inhale + exhale) takes a relaxed 8–15 seconds.
- Seven breaths = a wonderful little reset.
- No stopwatch needed. Just listen to your body's natural rhythm.

(xv) How long does it take to complete 7 deep breaths?
It depends on your breathing capacity and how long you take per breath. Typically, seven deep breaths take approximately one minute, but this can vary based on factors like your lung capacity, relaxation level and personal comfort.

(xvi) How long should each breath last?
A relaxed breath (inhale + exhale) usually takes between eight to fifteen seconds. This timing can vary depending on your current stress levels, physical activity, lung health and whether you include a breath hold.

(xvii) Do I hold my breath during breathing?
Yes, for breaths three to seven, as will be explained in the upcoming chapters, there is a brief pause after the inhale. This gentle pause helps deepen your awareness without causing any strain.

(xviii) Do I need a stopwatch to time my breaths?
No, you don't need a stopwatch. The best approach is to listen to your body's natural rhythm and breathe comfortably, adjusting to what feels right for you in the moment.

(xix) Can I still benefit if I don't have time for all seven breaths?
Absolutely. Even if you're pressed for time, you can still receive the benefits of this practice. Try the Mini Breath—the final three breaths from the full technique, which will take approximately

thirty seconds. This compact version helps you ground yourself quickly and can be especially useful before snacks or in on-the-go situations. With consistency, even the shortened version becomes a powerful tool for intentional eating.

I Practise, I Evolve

I know this path well. Until I was authoring wellness books, guiding dieticians with practical advice and mentoring people in fitness and well-being as a clinical wellness specialist at one of the leading and reputed hospitals in Mumbai, I was living it—fit, strong and in control of my health. But when I took on a business project in my family enterprise, my attention to a healthy lifestyle quietly began to slip.

One day, as I struggled to pull on my favourite pair of jeans, I had a wake-up call. Something needed to change—not just my weight, but my way of living. I needed a gentler, more sustainable approach. One that could blend into a busy professional life without guilt or extremes.

That's when I began developing my method. A way of eating and living that wasn't about restriction, but about reconnection. A practical system rooted in relaxed discipline—listening, pausing and responding to what the body truly needs.

This practice is the outcome of that journey.

It's my method, my inspiration, and the path that helped me return to my weight goals and my balance. I share this with you joyously—not as a rulebook, but as a quiet companion to your slimming goals.

These testimonials are such wonderful examples of the gentle power of this practice. What resonates most with me is the underlying theme of reconnection. For so long, my relationship with food felt dictated by what I thought I should do or by how I was feeling.

The 7 Breaths Practice became a way to quiet the noise and tune back into what my body was truly asking for. It's a gentle practice, but its impact on self-awareness—and ultimately, on eating habits—has been remarkable in my own life.

I believe these testimonials beautifully illustrate that same inner shift.

- **Nisha, corporate lawyer:** After intense meetings, I'd devour dinner. I wasn't hungry, just stressed. With this practice, I didn't change what I ate—just how much. I felt full faster, more satisfied and less regretful.
- **Nikhil, foodie:** I always went for a second helping, even when I wasn't hungry. With this practice, I'd stop, reflect and often skip round two. That pause became the difference between habit and intention.
- **Aparna, young mother:** I'd eat while feeding my child or checking my phone, and the food was gone, but I still felt empty. This practice helped me hear what my body was quietly saying: 'You've had enough.' I realized I was full halfway through. I didn't need to clean the plate.
- **Ravi, regular runner:** Training taught me discipline, but I never carried that into my meals. I used to binge after long runs, justifying it as fuel. This practice taught me to respect hunger, not reward it blindly. Now, I eat to nourish, not to compensate.
- **Meera, retired piano teacher:** I always believed that finishing my plate was respectful. But at 61, I was carrying unwanted weight and joint pain. This practice helped me break lifelong patterns with ease. I've lost

weight gently, and more importantly, I feel lighter in spirit.

This book, *7 Breaths to Slimming*, is about just that. To remember your goals. To know when enough is enough.

NamitaSpeaks

7 Breaths to Slimming is simply about taking a gentle pause to practise taking 7 Breaths before your meals—a tiny way to align with your slimming goals. If it feels like a lot at first, please ease into it, but do keep going. Eventually, it will become a natural rhythm for you. To experience the benefits, consistency is key. Practise before each meal, and with every breath, you'll gain a little more awareness. And that's truly where lasting change begins. With every breath, you're not just slimming—you're gently coming back to yourself.

2

The Power of Intention: Breath and Affirmation Ignite the Slimming Shift

Can seven focused breaths, paired with affirmations, really transform how you eat, feel and lose weight?

Every word we speak is an affirmation. Make them count.

—Louise Hay

Young and jovial graphic designer Jay was determined to lose weight, but wary of surgical and pharmaceutical options. He was sceptical about their success rate and apprehensive about possible side effects. His frustration peaked when he couldn't fit into a cherished shirt. Despite his doubts about conventional methods, Jay discovered an effective path to weight loss—and how! Hear him out.

'I used to snack during work breaks without even thinking. It wasn't hunger—it was just habit. Then I started practising 7 Breaths to Slimming before meals.' He had been watching a video on slimming where the speaker shared how he had benefited from the practice—a blend of breathwork and affirmations. It sounded simple enough to try.

He realized something powerful: the 7 Breaths Practice wasn't just about breathwork or affirmations. It's about how breath and thought work together—a powerful combination. This synergy is the key to lasting change, making slimming feel natural and effortless.

He continued, 'Breathing slowly and intentionally helped break the cycle of mindless eating. That small pause created space for awareness around food. Weight loss wasn't the only outcome—there was also a sense of clarity and control. The practice continues, grounded in faith and consistency. And now…my girlfriend says she needs seven Breaths just to handle how good I look!'

Jay's story reveals the real game-changer. Breath interrupted the habit of snacking aimlessly.

The 7 Breaths to Slimming Practice

You can say the affirmations aloud, softly or simply in your mind. What truly matters is the focused intention you bring to each breath.

Breaths 1 and 2: Gentle Arrival

- Inhale softly… Exhale gently…
- Inhale softly… Exhale gently… (These first two breaths are a quiet moment to arrive, to let go of any distractions and become present.)

Breaths 3, 4 and 5: Cultivating Inner Control

Inhale gently, hold briefly—silently affirm: 'Control'—exhale softly. Repeat three times. With these breaths, you gently cultivate a sense of inner discipline and conscious choice around your eating.

Your Anchors of Strength in Moments of Temptation

Breaths 6 and 7 are like gentle anchors, there to support you when you might feel challenged. They're not rigid rules, but kind reminders of the strength and intention you're building.

Breath 6: 'I Can Control'

Inhale gently through your nose. Pause briefly and silently affirm: 'I can control.'- Exhale softly. (This breath builds trust in your ability to make choices that align with your goals, reminding you that you can stop before feeling overly full and move away from old habits.)

Breath 7: 'I Will Control'

Inhale gently again. Pause briefly and affirm: 'I will control.' Exhale with intention. (This final breath is a gentle yet firm commitment to yourself, a promise to follow through with mindful and balanced eating.)

Why These Breaths Matter: A Simple Reflection

- Breaths 1 and 2—Relaxation: These first breaths are for relaxation. They calm your nervous system, slow your thoughts and ease you into a peaceful, receptive state.
- Breaths 3, 4 and 5—Discipline: These breaths are for discipline. Repeating the affirmation 'Control' reinforces your ability to make conscious, empowered choices in the moment.
- Breaths 6 and 7—Portion Control: These final breaths are for portion control. They anchor your intention to eat mindfully, helping you honour your body's signals and stop before feeling overly full.

As you move through this seven-breath sequence, notice how slow, intentional breathing activates your parasympathetic nervous system—the state of rest and digest. When combined with affirmations, you're not just breathing; you're sowing seeds of transformation in a calm, open mind. This allows your intentions to take root more deeply and naturally flourish.

When Breath Meets Thought: The Heart of 7 Breaths to Slimming

This practice, paired with affirmations, might sound unconvincing at first. But as you journey through the chapters, understand the science and experience the benefits for yourself, this pioneering practice transforms into an everyday mantra.

Addressing Scepticism about Affirmations

Now, you might be wondering if simply repeating words can truly make a difference. Think of it this way: the thoughts you consistently hold shape your reality. Affirmations are a tool to consciously direct those thoughts. By repeatedly stating positive intentions, you begin to override negative self-talk and ingrained patterns. This primes your subconscious mind to align with your goals, making healthier choices feel more natural over time.

Your internal GPS

Here's the crucial cue: Breath alone can ground you. A clear thought alone has potential, but both need focus as the fulcrum point of performance. When combined, this is the crux of the matter—they align to form a formidable force of intention.

It acts like your internal GPS, reshaping your mindset and guiding you towards your slimming goals, making 7 Breaths to Slimming a stunning success.

Wait—is this really about slimming

At first, the idea of 7 Breaths to Slimming might sound too simple. You might even think, I've tried more complicated techniques before, and they didn't work.

You Might Wonder: Can It Be This Easy?

The answer is: it's not just about ease—it's about alignment. When your breath and thoughts sync, your decisions start to change effortlessly.

But here's the difference: this approach isn't about mastering complex breathing exercises or following strict rituals. It's about the power of simplicity—just seven breaths, combined with intention. This synergy is the key to lasting change, making slimming a natural and effortless process. Simplicity isn't the opposite of effectiveness—it's the secret to effortless transformation.

Why Does 7 Breaths to Slimming Work So Effectively?

Before we dive into the science, pause and reflect: Have you ever found yourself eating, not out of hunger, but out of habit, stress or emotion? You're not alone. Whether it's the late-night snack, the bored bites between meetings or finishing a plate just because it's there, unconscious eating is more common than we realize.

Jay's story was one example, but this practice can help anyone, at any stage of life, break the autopilot loop. Like Meera, a 42-year-old working mom, who shared: 'Taking those seven breaths gave me back my pause. I didn't realise how rushed and reactive my eating had become. It wasn't just about food—it was about reconnecting with myself.'

These moments of awareness are what truly change the game.

It works because it combines two powerful elements:

1. **Your Nervous System:** Activating the parasympathetic (rest-and-digest) mode helps calm stress and reduces impulsive eating.
2. **Your Mindset:** Affirmations build discipline, replacing self-sabotage with intentional eating. This pre-meal pause fosters awareness, not autopilot. Slimming starts with seven breaths, aligning your energy with your goals, guiding you to choose wisely and release negativity.

Wonder How Slimming Happens?

Each breath is a small but powerful step toward regaining control. When practised consistently, those seven breaths paired with affirmations create a force that helps you make wise decisions in the moments that matter most. This daily practice calms cravings, clears your mind and supports portion control—the foundation of sustainable slimming. There are no complex techniques or restrictive rules. Over time, it transforms from a simple habit into your most trusted ally in making smarter decisions.

As you can see, this isn't just another diet or pep talk. It's the synergy that awakens you to make the crucial choices for slimming. Your breath calms and centres you, while your thoughts focus and direct your mind, together creating new habits that guide you towards your goals.

So, What Are Affirmations?

Affirmations are much more than just words—they're a direct conversation with your mind. Your subconscious is where habits are formed, while your conscious mind makes those active decisions. When you pair affirmations with your breath, they help you break free from old patterns like emotional eating and cravings, making space for healthier habits.

How Do Affirmations Affect the Mind?

When you affirm your slimming goals, your subconscious takes them as truth, wiping away past guilt and negative self-images. This shift empowers you to make healthier choices. At the same time, affirmations activate your conscious mind, allowing you to pause and make thoughtful, intentional decisions. It's the best of both worlds—mind and body working together.

How the Process Works

With just seven breaths, you shift from stress to focus. As you breathe, your affirmations send a powerful message: *I can control. I will control.*

For example, imagine you're about to face a stressful lunch meeting or feel a sudden craving for a snack. Taking a moment to pause, breathe and repeat your affirmations anchors you in the present, calming your nervous system and shifting your focus from stress or impulse to intention.

This simple yet effective loop rewires your brain, making slimming feel effortless and natural—not a struggle.

'I have the willpower.'

'I am focused on my goals.'

'I nourish my body with awareness.'

Once you've become comfortable with these initial affirmations, feel free to adapt them to resonate even more deeply with your personal goals and challenges. The key is to keep them positive, present tense and focused on what you want to achieve. Remember, like any positive habit, the power of 7 Breaths to Slimming and its affirmations grows with consistent daily practice. Even taking those few moments before each meal will compound over time.

NamitaSpeaks

Weight loss can be a process that unfolds naturally, with each breath and intention guiding you towards lasting results. These seven breaths aren't just a pause before meals; they're a reset. Each breath calms your cravings. Each affirmation strengthens your resolve. Over time, this simple practice becomes your inner compass, guiding you to eat not out of habit, but out of harmony with your goals. Remember—missing a day or two doesn't undo your progress. The power of the practice grows over time, not in perfection. Each mindful pause reinforces your connection to your body and your intentions.

3

Breaths 1 and 2: Breathing into Calm

You're about to eat, but your mind is racing elsewhere. Sounds familiar?

'The real miracle isn't walking on water. It's walking on the green earth, fully alive and rooted in the present moment.'

—Thich Nhat Hanh

In today's world, we are pulled in a hundred different directions. Yet being fully present, free of distractions and judgements, is essential for peace of mind and health. This is where 7 Breaths to Slimming begins.

In this chapter, we delve into the first principle of 7 Breaths to Slimming: relaxation. It's about cultivating a calm, relaxed state before eating—crucial for better digestion, slimming and inner balance.

Maintain a slow and gentle rhythm with each breath. Even amidst chaos, Breaths one and two draw you back to the present, reconnecting you with your body before your first bite. It's not just about slowing down—it's about eating with purpose and presence.

The Invisible Weight: Stress

Here's something to think about:

I once came across a quote on a social media post:

One goldfish turns to another and says, 'How's the water?' The other replies, 'What the heck is water?'

It's a simple reminder: sometimes, we are so used to living with stress that we don't even notice it anymore.

Stress becomes the background noise of our lives—silent but exhausting. First step? Notice it. Acknowledge its presence. Only then can you loosen its grip, reclaim your focus and recharge your energy.

Why Relaxation Changes Everything

Even the healthiest meal can cause discomfort if eaten in a state of stress. When you're rushed or tense, you chew less, digest poorly and often experience bloating, heaviness or unease.

It's not just about what's on your plate—it's about how you receive your meal. When you eat with peace, gratitude and happiness, your food nourishes and heals you from within.

If you're tense, your body holds on to weight. Stress disrupts digestion, nutrient absorption and appetite regulation. Breaths one and two help you reset your state before the first bite. Slimming begins not on your plate, but in your mind.

Stress Wears Many Masks

At mealtimes, stress looks different for everyone:

- A parent eats between diaper changes.
- A student crunching chips while studying.

- A professional inhaling lunch during a Zoom call.
- A heartbroken soul mindlessly devouring chocolate.

Different stories. Same pattern. Breaths one and two invite you to press the pause button—Just long enough to notice, breathe and shift from reactive to intentional eating. That's where transformation begins.

The Mindset You Bring to the Table Matters

How you show up to your meal shapes everything—your hunger, your choices, your satisfaction. It affects more than just your appetite. It influences how much you eat and how you feel afterwards. Before your mind races ahead or your phone pulls you into distractions, take a pause to breathe.

Instead of getting lost in memories of a recent vacation or a special gift from your spouse, you'll start tuning in to your body's hunger cues.

You'll savour each bite, feel satisfied and support your digestion. You'll focus on what you truly need, not on fleeting cravings.

When your mind is relaxed, portion control becomes effortless. Slimming becomes simpler and consistency follows naturally. Weight loss becomes inevitable. Regular practice of the 7 Breaths to Slimming doesn't just promote weight loss—it transforms your life. It empowers you to make mindful, disciplined choices that lead to lasting change.

Relax First, Slim Later

Breaths one and two quiet your mind and soften your body. When you relax, everything shifts:

- Digestion improves.
- Metabolism stabilizes.
- Your body exits 'fight-or-flight' and enters 'rest-and-digest' mode. This is the state where real nourishment—and real change—begins.

Science Reveals the Truth: Relax to Reset

Your body listens to both your mood and your meal. When you're stressed, cortisol levels rise, signalling your brain to crave sugar, salt and fat. But when you pause to breathe before eating, cortisol levels drop, and appetite hormones like ghrelin and leptin find their balance. The result? You eat with more ease, digest better, and feel satisfied, not stuffed. A calm state doesn't just soothe your mind—it supports lasting weight loss from the inside out.

The Snacking Trap (and How to Beat It)

Ever noticed how relaxed settings often lead to mindless snacking? Chips, fries, nuts...a bite here, a handful there. It's not about guilt—it's about staying focused. Being relaxed and aware makes all the difference. A simple breath before your first bite can change everything. Breaths one and two are simply about breathing and clearing your mind.

Take Sarah, a newly married host. At a recent gathering, she paused to breathe before going towards the snack table. Instead of slipping into autopilot, she stayed present. She still enjoyed her chips, but with clear intention. She knew her goals and stayed on track. The result? She felt satisfied, not stuffed, and the evening remained light and joyful.

Mindless snacking can contribute to weight gain, but

when you're relaxed and in control, a few treats won't derail your slimming journey. Staying calm doesn't kill the vibe—it enhances the joy and keeps you on track.

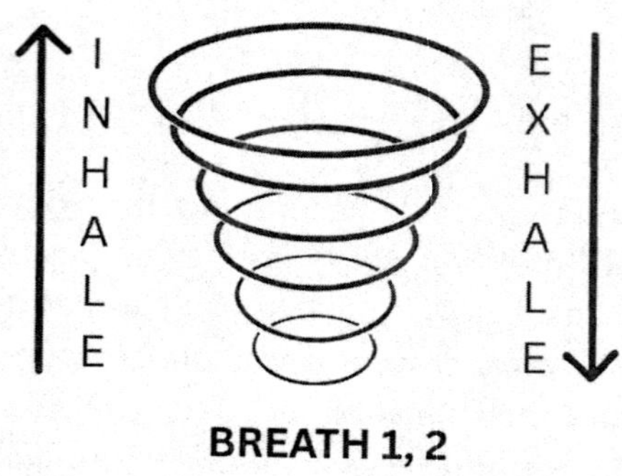

BREATH 1, 2

Breaths 1 and 2: Your Foundation of Calm

The first two breaths in the 7 Breaths to Slimming practice embody the core principle of relaxation. Simple yet powerful, they invite you to pause, breathe and reset. With these two breaths, you set the stage for transformation—one breath at a time.

Breath 1: The Relaxation Breath

- Inhale gently through your nose (taking approximately four to seven seconds).
- Exhale fully through your mouth, as if you're letting out a soft sigh (taking approximately four to seven seconds).
- Let go and arrive in the moment.

Breath 2: The Deeper Relaxation Breath

- Inhale again, letting your breath settle deeper into your body (taking approximately four to seven seconds).
- Exhale slowly, releasing tension from your shoulders, jaw and belly (taking approximately four to seven seconds).
- Feel yourself soften and relax even more.

These first two breaths lay the groundwork for the affirmations we'll introduce starting with Breath 3. By first cultivating this sense of calm and presence, we create a more receptive state for our intentions to take root.

Why a Soft Sigh?

A soft sigh triggers your body's natural relaxation response. It eases tension, shifts you into 'rest-and-digest' mode, and helps you focus, stay calm and make better choices. It signals your nervous system to relax and stay in control.

Posture Tip

- Sit comfortably with your spine upright but relaxed.
- You can close your eyes or soften your gaze.
- Inhale through your nose and exhale through your mouth—or your nose, if that feels better.
- Relax your shoulders. Unclench your jaw. Feel your body let go.

That's it for now. Simply breathe, relax and arrive.

Note: Affirmations will come next with Breath Three—because presence comes before intention. For now, just permit yourself to be.

NamitaSpeaks

Breaths 1 and 2: A Recap

- Inhale... Exhale...
- Inhale... Exhale...
- Relaxation isn't a luxury—it's your first step towards slimming. Start each meal with calm and clarity.

Up Next: Breaths 3, 4 and 5

4

Breaths 3, 4 and 5: Breathing into Discipline

Without self-discipline, success is impossible, period.
—Lou Holtz.

Pretty straightforward, right?

Think about anything you've truly wanted and achieved. Whether it was those few stubborn kilos you finally shed, excelling in a sport, nailing that challenging yoga pose, sticking to your morning walks, learning a new language or a skill, or even just making it to that early flight—what was the quiet force behind it all? You got it—discipline. It's the unsung hero in every success story, wouldn't you agree?

Discipline isn't about turning into some rigid rule-follower for everyone else; it's about becoming the master of yourself, making those small but significant decisions, one at a time.

Take Lou Holtz, the legendary football coach and author. He didn't just rely on star players to transform underdog teams. It was his relentless focus on discipline and unwavering belief that turned the tide. His career? A powerful reminder of what consistent effort and inner control can achieve.

And let's be honest, is there any area where our discipline gets tested more than when we're aiming for health and weight goals?

The world throws a constant barrage of quick fixes our way, doesn't it? Fad diets, fancy gadgets, miracle pills, all promising lightning-fast results. It's so tempting, especially when you're eager to see those stubborn pounds disappear. And sure, some might offer a temporary boost, maybe even work for a little while.

But here's the truth that's rarely emphasized: without discipline, nothing lasts. Even the most brilliant plan will crumble if our discipline wavers. And when it does, those old habits? They sneak right back in, often bringing the weight with them, sometimes even faster and more stubbornly than before. Ever experienced that?

I Practise, I Evolve

Take Sheena, a vibrant woman in her late twenties. She loved her weekend social scene, those delicious but often indulgent dinners. But every Monday felt like a setback—the bloating, the guilt, that annoying feeling of being off-track. After those post-wedding kilos crept in, she knew something had to shift.

That's when she found 7 Breaths to Slimming. Sheena liked the concept and started practising those seven breaths before every meal. But she told me it was breaths three, four, and five that clicked for her. It introduced her to this quiet, often underestimated strength: discipline.

Instead of feeling like she was constantly denying herself, she felt empowered, making those wiser choices almost effortlessly. Those weekend weight fluctuations? They stopped, and then the scale started moving in the right direction. Her slimming goals became clearer; her energy felt more consistent. And her mindset? Seriously stronger.

And guess what? People around her noticed! 'Wait—you're just breathing before you eat? That sounds doable!' her friends would exclaim. Inspired by Sheena's success, they jumped on the breath-powered eating bandwagon too, rediscovering a sense of freedom, joy and wisdom around food.

Discipline isn't about saying 'no' to everything enjoyable; it's about aligning your actions with what you truly want. And in 7 Breaths to Slimming, discipline starts right with your breath. Each pause isn't about white-knuckling your way through cravings; it's about creating a space for clarity and conscious choice. With every breath, you're gently but firmly realigning with your deepest goals—calmly, confidently and with intention.

In a world obsessed with those quick fixes, the real secret to lasting change lies in nurturing that discipline from within. Sure, you can try the latest trend with a swipe of your card. But when the initial excitement fades, what's left? True transformation, the kind that lasts, doesn't come through shortcuts.

Whether you choose to explore other slimming tools is totally up to you; there's no right or wrong answer here. But if you want results that you can count on—long-term—there's one constant you can always rely on: good old discipline. It's not flashy, it's not glamorous, but it's steady, it's empowering, and guess what? It's already within you.

Breaths 3, 4 and 5: Grounding through Breath

After those first two relaxing breaths helped you find your calm and centre your mind, it's time to tap into your inner powerhouse: discipline. Breaths three, four and five are like your internal reset button, helping you shift from just reacting to making intentional choices. With each of these breaths, we're going to gently affirm one powerful word: Control.

Think of it as your anchor, a steady reminder of what you want to achieve and your amazing ability to choose. Breath by breath, you'll find yourself moving away from those unconscious reactions and towards a place of conscious clarity. And trust me, that's where the real magic of change begins.

The Principle of Discipline: Freedom through Awareness

In 7 Breaths to Slimming, discipline isn't some heavy, restrictive force. It's actually about creating more freedom for yourself through greater awareness. Think about it—true discipline isn't about deprivation; it's about consciously choosing what truly serves you in the long run. It's the subtle power behind every real achievement. Consider:

- A painter who shows up at his easel day after day, honing his craft.
- A musician who diligently practises those scales and notes
- A chef who keeps experimenting and refining recipes, one step at a time.
- A business owner who makes those consistent, sometimes unexciting, decisions to grow his business.

Across every field—art, sports, business, wellness—the people who truly thrive don't just rely on fleeting motivation. They build their success on the foundation of discipline. You don't need to be perfect; you just need to keep showing up, breath by breath.

Breathing Builds Control: It's Science!

Ever notice how, when things get stressful, someone will often say, 'Just take a deep breath'? It's not just some comforting saying—there's actual neuroscience behind it! Research shows that when you breathe consciously, you're activating your prefrontal cortex—the part of your brain responsible for judgement, decision-making and willpower. So, when you breathe with intention, you're doing more than just calming down; you're strengthening your brain's ability to pause, think things through and make wiser choices.

That's a big part of why this technique works. With every breath, you're gently but decisively retraining your brain to respond thoughtfully to situations instead of reacting automatically.

Each of these three breaths follows a simple rhythm:

- Inhale (slowly and gently through your nose)
- Hold (briefly, allowing the affirmation to resonate) and affirm: 'Control.'
- Exhale (softly through your mouth)

In that little moment of stillness during the breath-hold, you're reminding yourself: you have a choice. Every single time.

The Biology behind Cravings: Understanding Ghrelin

Let's talk about cravings for a second. You're not weak for experiencing them—you're wired for it! When your stomach is empty, it releases this hormone called ghrelin—often called the 'hunger hormone'—and it sends a pretty strong message to your brain: 'Eat now!' But here's the thing: ghrelin doesn't just spike when you're truly hungry. It also surges when you're feeling stressed, sleep-deprived or even just when you see or smell something delicious.

That's why you sometimes feel ravenous even when your body doesn't need fuel. This is where breaths three, four and five become your allies. They help you create a little space to manage those powerful triggers, allowing your logical, thinking brain to step in and guide your next move.

Science Snapshot: Breath vs. Ghrelin

- Ghrelin levels naturally rise before meals, signalling hunger.
- Stress and not enough sleep can cause ghrelin to spike even higher.
- The good news? Deep breathing helps reduce cortisol (that pesky stress hormone), which in turn can help balance ghrelin.
- Bottom line: each mindful breath you take helps you regain a little bit more control.

These Breaths Matter: Your Secret Weapon

Think of these three breaths as your secret superpower, ready to be deployed exactly when you need it most:

- When stress, boredom or your emotions are whispering sweet nothings about that fridge.
- When you find yourself reaching for that second (or maybe even third) helping, even though you know you're not truly hungry anymore.
- When you feel yourself about to veer off-track from the goals you've set for yourself.

Instead of just diving in on autopilot, you now have this incredible tool: pause, breathe and hit that internal reset button. It's like saying, 'Wait a minute, I'm in control here.'

Breath-by-Breath Guide: Your Moment of Choice

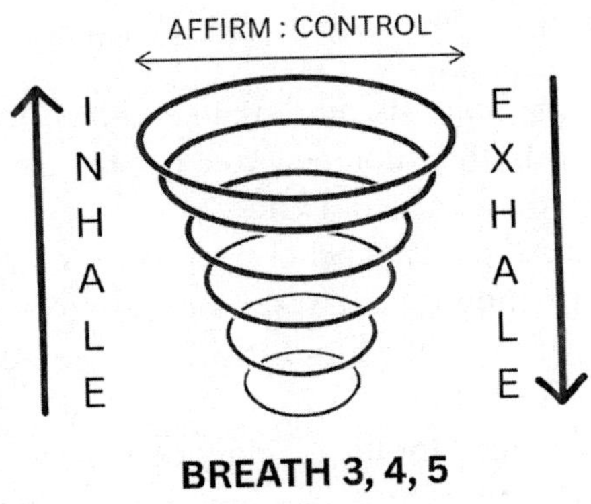

BREATH 3, 4, 5

Remember, you can say the affirmation silently to yourself or softly aloud—whatever feels most present and intentional for you.

- **Breath 3:** Inhale slowly and gently through your nose. Hold briefly, allowing the affirmation 'Control' to resonate within you. Exhale softly through your mouth.
- **Breath 4:** Inhale gently again. Hold briefly, focusing on that inner voice affirming 'Control'. Exhale, releasing any tension you might be holding.
- **Breath 5:** Inhale deeply once more, filling your lungs. Hold, firmly affirming 'Control' to yourself. Exhale fully, and feel a sense of calm and release wash over you.

Posture tip: Sit comfortably with your spine upright yet relaxed. Let your shoulders drop naturally. Soften your gaze or gently close your eyes. Inhale through your nose, and exhale through your mouth with a soft sigh (or through your nose, if that feels more natural).

Inhale. Hold. Affirm—Control. Exhale.

The pause—the hold—is more than stillness. It's a deliberate act of control. In that moment, you are not just holding your breath but holding your awareness.

It becomes a space to anchor your intention, to affirm your power, and to choose your response rather than react. This simple practice trains the mind to pause, observe and act with intention.

And by repeating the breath practice with the affirmation—'Control'—three times, the message gently seeps in, inviting discipline to take root in your mind.

NamitaSpeaks

Breaths 3, 4, and 5: .A Recap

- Inhale…
- Hold (briefly). Affirm: 'Control'.
- Exhale…

Repeat this sequence three times before you eat. Remember, discipline is your inner compass, guiding you towards your goals. These three breaths are a powerful way to align your actions with your slimming intentions.

Let's reflect:

- Breaths 1 and 2—Relaxation: setting the stage for calm and presence.
- Breaths 3, 4 and 5—Discipline: empowering conscious choices and inner control.

Up Next: Breaths 6 and 7

5

Breaths 6 and 7: The Portion Control Breaths

Small servings sharpen the appetite.

—Inspired by French Wisdom

How do you turn those little moments of temptation—that extra bite, that second helping—into powerful acts of self-control?

French culinary wisdom reminds us that true satisfaction isn't about overindulging, but about restraint. This chapter dives into portion control—a simple yet profound habit that can completely reshape your relationship with food. It's not about eliminating your favourite meals; it's about understanding how much your body needs. And that's where 7 Breaths to Slimming steps in, empowering you to pause, really assess what's going on, and choose with awareness.

The Principle of Portion Control: The Real Game-Changer

Ever notice how just a few extra bites, those seemingly insignificant amounts, can subtly tip the scale, whether it's towards feeling guilty or hindering your progress?

You're not alone if thoughts like these have crossed your mind:

- 'It's just a tiny treat—what harm can it do?'
- 'I deserve this—I've had such a long day.'
- 'I hate wasting food, so I might as well just finish it.'

These moments? They're so familiar. They often nudge us off our path without us even fully realizing it. But here's the encouraging news: even the smallest, most consistent shifts in how much you eat can lead to significant and lasting changes in the long run.

In a world of super-sized portions and social pressures to 'clean your plate', it's easy for external cues to override your body's subtle signals. The beauty of the breath practice is its ability to re-centre you on your internal wisdom, helping you make choices based on your body's true needs, rather than what's on your plate or expected of you.

The Eighty Per Cent Fullness Rule: Your Sweet Spot for Sustainable Slimming

Learning to stop at around eighty per cent fullness, not quite full, but comfortably satisfied—is a cornerstone of sustainable slimming. This may feel unfamiliar at first; after all, eating until completely full is a deeply ingrained habit for many.

The 7 Breaths Practice, particularly breaths six and seven, becomes your key tool in making this shift. It helps you tune in to your body's true signals, allowing you to pause and stop before reaching the point of feeling overly stuffed. It's about finding that 'sweet spot'—a skill that develops gradually with conscious practice. Over time, this new way of eating becomes second nature, creating space for lightness, renewed energy and lasting change.

Controlled Eating: The Hidden Habit behind Natural Slimness

We all know that slimming down often comes down to portion control. But in the heat of the moment, when that delicious food is right in front of you, it can feel almost impossible to put on the brakes! That's the real challenge, isn't it?

So, what's the trick? It's about outsmarting that immediate urge before it takes over. Remind yourself gently: there's almost always more tomorrow. You can save some for later—it's not going anywhere. That fleeting pleasure of overeating so rarely outweighs the lasting discomfort (and those extra pounds that seem to stick around).

And here's what science backs up: individuals who naturally maintain a lean physique often share this powerful habit—they intuitively stop eating before they feel full.

This principle is not limited to one culture, either. While the Japanese concept of Hara Hachi Bu—eating until you're about eighty per cent full—is often talked about, similar wisdom exists across the globe. In Ayurvedic tradition, it's recommended that you leave about one-third of your stomach empty to aid digestion.

In Mediterranean regions, meals are often enjoyed slowly and in social settings, usually with smaller portions of nutrient-dense foods, naturally encouraging moderation without the feeling of being restricted.

Across different cultures and solid scientific studies, one key theme emerges: it's not about deprivation or restriction, but about truly knowing when to say, 'Ok, that's enough for now.'

The Science behind Portion Control

Could how much you're eating be the real reason your healthy efforts haven't paid off as expected, more so than what you're eating?

It could be that seemingly small indulgence of a silky spoonful of dessert after dinner, that extra handful of nuts while you're watching TV—the point is to enjoy just enough to feel genuinely content, not feeling compelled to keep eating until you're stuffed.

Whatever's on your plate, the core principle remains: aim to stop before you're full. That's the sweet spot—where you feel satisfied and energized, not heavy and sluggish. And when you make this a consistent way of eating, you'll likely feel lighter, more energized throughout the day and more in tune with what your body is telling you.

Tune in to Your Body's 'Enough' Signals

So, how do you know when you've eaten just enough and are approaching that 'eighty per cent full' point? It's simpler than you might think: if you consistently feel heavy, sluggish or like you need a nap right after your meal, chances are, you've gone past what your body truly needed. Pay attention to those subtle cues of satisfaction, that gentle feeling of 'enough'.

It doesn't matter if you're following keto, embracing a vegan lifestyle, avoiding gluten, or trying the latest health trend—portion control is often the unsung hero.

Food is meant to fuel you, to lift you up, not to leave you feeling weighed down. The real goal is sustained energy, not uncomfortable excess.

Wondering if you're getting better at listening to your body's cues? Here's a little test you can do after eating:

The Lightness Test: Portion Control

- You feel comfortably satisfied and energetic.
- You can take a deep breath without any discomfort in your stomach.
- You still feel relatively light and alert after eating, not like you need to crash on the sofa.
- You could easily go for a light walk or do some gentle stretching without feeling weighed down.
- You feel genuinely content, not still craving more food.

Sure, we all know the basic advice: eat less, move more. But if it were truly that easy, we wouldn't keep finding ourselves in those frustrating cycles—yo-yo dieting, feeling discouraged and searching for those quick fixes that never seem to last.

I hear it all the time: 'I eat pretty healthy! I watch what I eat!' And yet…the struggle often continues. Why? Because it's not just about occasionally eating less. It's about staying consistently connected to your breath, your body's signals and even your emotions.

And that's what's so beautiful about 7 Breaths to Slimming. It's not another rigid diet rulebook. It's a rhythm, a simple practice that gently brings you back to yourself, again and again, meal after meal.

Aligning with Slimming: Finding Your Natural Balance

When you start to live in tune with your body's natural hunger, when you take that moment to pause, breathe and truly listen, you'll likely find yourself naturally stopping around that eighty per cent full mark. You won't have to obsessively measure, meticulously count calories or constantly stress about every single bite. You'll simply feel…'Enough!'

The real beauty of the 7 Breaths to Slimming practice is that it's not just about what you eat; it's deeply about how you engage with your food and, more importantly, with your own body. It's about creating a calm, centred space before you even pick up your fork. This simple rhythm helps you make decisions that truly align with your long-term goals, rather than just reacting to those immediate cravings or emotional urges.

And when you consistently hit that right spot of comfortable satisfaction, everything starts to shift: the weight can begin to release more naturally, your energy levels often improve, and the results?

You start to feel good in both your mind and your body, more determined in your resolve and great in your skin.

A Lasting Change: It's about 'Enough', Not Less

What if the real secret to feeling lighter, more energized and truly in control isn't about drastically eating less, but about consistently eating just the right amount—enough to nourish you, but not so much that you feel weighed down?

Portion control isn't some trendy, new wellness fad; it's a timeless and incredibly effective tool. It's not about forcing yourself to finish every last morsel on your plate or mindlessly grazing your way through an entire TV show. It's about cultivating that deep connection with your body and learning to listen when it gently whispers, 'I've had enough now.'

By consistently aiming to stop around that eighty per cent full point, you'll naturally start to dodge that uncomfortable bloating, that post-meal fatigue and that nagging food guilt. You'll likely feel lighter, more energized throughout your day and more in control of your eating habits.

Remember, it's not about harsh restriction; it's about mindful focus. And once you truly embrace this way of eating, you might just find you never want to go back to that overstuffed feeling. Plus, taking good care of your health and feeling great often leads to a natural confidence that others can sense. So, whether you're at a party, enjoying a staycation or a guest at someone's home, portion control can become an effortless and natural part of how you enjoy your food.

Why These Breaths Matter: Your Anchors in Moments of Temptation

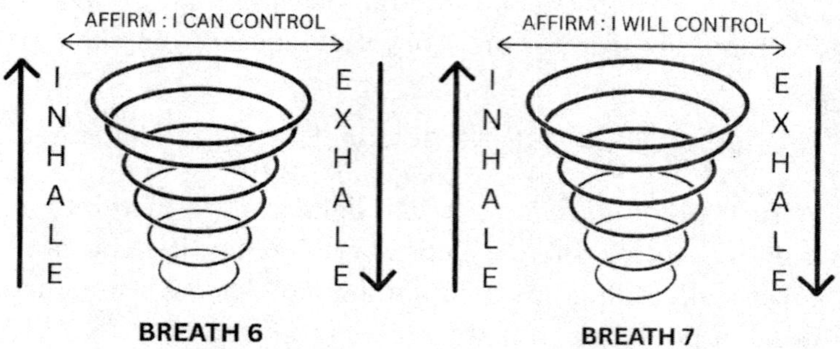

Breaths six and seven serve as your intuitive anchors, those reliable tools you can turn to, especially in moments when temptation might arise. They aren't strict, unyielding rules—they're more like gentle, supportive reminders that you've got this.

- **Breath 6—'I Can Control':** Inhale deeply and gently through your nose. Hold that breath for a moment and silently affirm to yourself: 'I can control.' Exhale softly through your mouth. (This breath is all about building trust in yourself, reinforcing the powerful idea that you absolutely can stop eating before you feel overly full. It's a reminder that you have the inner strength to change those old habits.)

- **Breath 7– 'I Will Control':** Inhale gently again. Hold that breath and affirm with intention: 'I will control'. Exhale with purpose. (This breath is like committing yourself, a gentle but firm promise that you will follow through with mindful and controlled eating. It's about solidifying your intention.).

Inhale. Hold. Affirm. Exhale.

The pause—the hold—is more than stillness. It's a moment of control and awareness, where you choose your response instead of reacting. By holding your breath, you anchor your intention and reclaim your power. This simple practice trains the mind to pause, choose and respond with intention.

These aren't just words—they're active affirmations that engage both mind and body. When you inhale and hold your breath during Breath Six and silently affirm '*I CAN control*', followed by '*I WILL control*' during Breath Seven, you're activating the prefrontal cortex—the area of the brain responsible for conscious choice and impulse control.

This moment of pause disrupts automatic behaviour, allowing you to step back, resist the urge to overeat and reconnect with your body's natural signals. This mental recalibration allows you to pause before reaching for that extra bite, strengthening your resolve and fostering a deep trust in your body's innate wisdom about what is truly 'enough'.

And here's a little tip: if you find yourself mid-meal feeling an urge to keep eating beyond comfortable fullness, don't hesitate to revisit these breaths. They can act as a mini reset, helping you tune back into your body's signals.

With consistent practice, your body will likely start to naturally signal when it's had enough. You'll begin to experience that gentle sense of satisfaction, rather than that heavy, uncomfortable feeling of being stuffed.

Posture Tip

Find a comfortable seat, let your shoulders relax and either close your eyes gently or soften your gaze. Breathe slowly and deeply. Unclench your jaw. Take a moment to turn inward and feel that quiet stillness within you.

I Practise, I Evolve

For years, Joseph, a Marketing Strategist, had this ingrained post-lunch habit of indulging in a variety of chocolates and desserts. It seemed like a small, harmless pleasure at first, but over time, those extra bites really added up—and so did the numbers on the scale. That's when he heard about 7 Breaths to Slimming from a colleague who had successfully lost weight without feeling like they were constantly missing out.

Intrigued, Joseph decided to give it a try. Before each meal, he started taking that pause for the 7 Breaths Practice, and something interesting happened: portion control started to feel almost automatic. Instead of mindlessly reaching for an entire box of chocolates, he found himself truly savouring just one piece, making it a genuine treat.

The result? He started losing weight without feeling like

he was saying goodbye to his favourite indulgences forever. It wasn't about strict elimination; it was all about consciously controlling what was on his plate. And as his body gradually adjusted, eating less actually became his new normal, without that nagging sense of deprivation.

This simple practice helped Joseph reconnect with his body's natural needs, creating a lasting awareness around food that continues to serve him well.

Careful Eating Cues: Simple Tweaks for Thoughtful Portions

Want to naturally eat less without constantly having to think about it? Here are a few simple and effective tweaks you can try incorporating into your routine:

- **Smaller Plates**: It's a clever mind trick! Your brain tends to perceive a fuller plate as a satisfying meal, even if the plate itself is smaller. Try downsizing your dinnerware.
- **The Pause Test (Mid-Meal):** While you're eating, take a brief moment to check in with yourself: 'Am I still truly hungry, or am I just enjoying the taste and the moment?' This little pause can be surprisingly effective in helping you stop before you've overeaten. And remember, you can even use breaths six and seven during this pause as a mini reset!
- **Restaurant Hack:** When you're eating out, consider sharing a dish with someone or asking the server to pack up half of your meal before you even start eating. You'll likely end up eating less and feel much better afterwards.

NamitaSpeaks

A Recap: Your Anchors for Portion Control

- Breath 6: Inhale… 'I can control'… Exhale.
- Breath 7: Inhale… 'I will control'… Exhale.

Breaths six and seven are your powerful anchors for portion control, enabling you to consciously choose 'just enough' and align with your body's true signals. This consistent practice cultivates inner discipline, leading to sustainable slimming and a harmonious relationship with food.

Let's reflect:

- Breaths 1 and 2—Relaxation: Setting the stage for calm and presence.
- Breaths 3, 4 and 5—Discipline: Empowering conscious choices and inner control.
- Breaths 6 and 7—The principle of portion control.

6

7 Breaths to Slimming: At a Glance

By now, you know the 7 Breaths Practice works. You've experienced its power to reshape habits, calm cravings and bring clarity. Keep this chapter handy! It's your quick guide and calming touchpoint—use it to realign with your goals before meals or snacks. (And yes, there's even a time-saving version ahead for those extra-hectic days—because we all need a shortcut sometimes.)

Before You Begin

- Sit upright, spine tall yet relaxed.
- Close your eyes—or keep them soft and open.
- Inhale through the nose.
- Exhale through the mouth, like a soft sigh (prefer nose exhale? That works too).
- Drop your shoulders, unclench your jaw, and turn inwards.

Why a Soft Sigh?

It activates the body's natural relaxation response, easing tension and switching on your 'rest-and-digest' mode. This supports better focus, balance and decision-making. It's your breath cue for calm and control.

The 7 Breaths Practice

You can say the affirmations aloud, softly or in your mind. What matters most is your intention.

Breaths 1 and 2: Just Breathe (Your moment to arrive and find calm.)

- Inhale… Exhale…
- Inhale… Exhale… (No affirmations—just arrive.)

Breaths 3, 4 and 5: Affirm: 'Control' (Cultivating inner discipline and conscious choice.)

- Inhale, hold—Affirm: 'Control'—Exhale (×3)

Breath 6: Affirm: 'I can control.' (Building trust in your ability to stop before fullness.)

- Inhale, hold—Affirm: 'I can control'—Exhale

Breath 7: Affirm: 'I will control' (committing to thoughtful and controlled eating).

- Inhale, Hold—Affirm: 'I will control'—Exhale

Remember: Once you feel comfortable with these core affirmations, adapt them to words that resonate even more deeply with your personal goals and challenges.

Time: 1 Minute

Seven breaths typically take about one minute, though this may vary slightly depending on factors like your lung capacity, level of relaxation and personal breathing rhythm.

Key Pointers

- Takes approximately 1 minute. (7 Breaths ≈ 1 minute)
- Each breath (inhale + exhale) takes a relaxed eight to fifteen seconds.
- Seven breaths = a wonderful reset.
- No stopwatch needed. Just listen to your body's natural rhythm.

When to Practise

- Before meals
- Before snacks
- Anytime you feel emotionally triggered to eat

Make It a Habit

1. **Pair with a cue:** Just after opening your tiffin or placing your napkin.
2. **Visual reminders:** Notes on the fridge, lunchbox, mirror or phone: 'Pause. 7 Breaths.'
3. **Snack smart:** Don't skip the breath just because it's 'just a snack'.
4. **Make it a family practice:** Kids and teens will also benefit from it.
5. **Use it anywhere:** Eating out? No one will notice—but you'll feel the difference.
6. **Missed the breath practice?** Begin again. Perfection isn't required—progress is.

Now, here's a surprise! By now, you've understood the 7 Breaths to Slimming practice—but I also want to leave you with another quicker option. The reason is that I am so convinced of this path to slimming that I want it to be as easy as possible for you to follow.

Remember, even a few intentional breaths are better than none. Don't let the pursuit of perfection prevent you from practising it altogether.

Introducing: The Mini Breath

In a rush or caught in a snacking spiral? Try the Mini Breath practice. Just three breaths—about thirty seconds—is all it takes to interrupt the pattern and reconnect with your intention. It's a shortcut to the full 7 Breaths Practice, using only the final three—each packed with the power of conscious control.

Why introduce it now and not earlier? Because shortcuts work best once you know the full path. The Mini Breath practice isn't a replacement—it's your reset button, perfect for those in-between moments: stress scrolling, boredom bites or mindless snacking.

We'll dive into the Mini Breath in the following chapter—step by step.

NamitaSpeaks

The 7 Breaths Practice puts you in the driver's seat—your power pause before every meal. It helps you slow down, reconnect and align with your slimming goals. Let it be your steady anchor.

Use the Mini Breath practice when needed—especially during rushed or in-between moments—but don't skip the full practice when time allows.

Remember it's consistency, not perfection, that creates real, lasting change.

Your breath—and your body—will thank you.

7 BREATHS

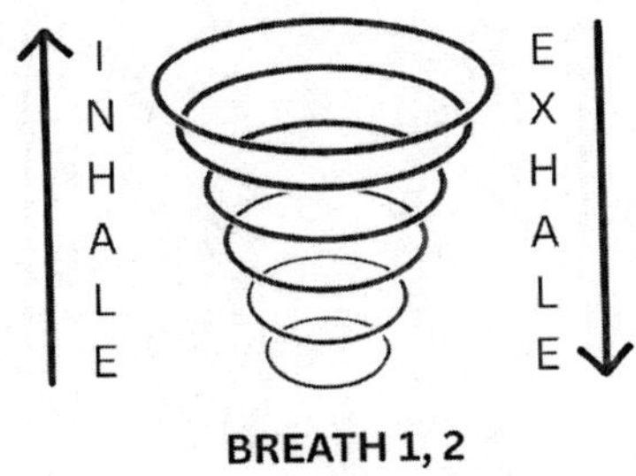

BREATH 1, 2

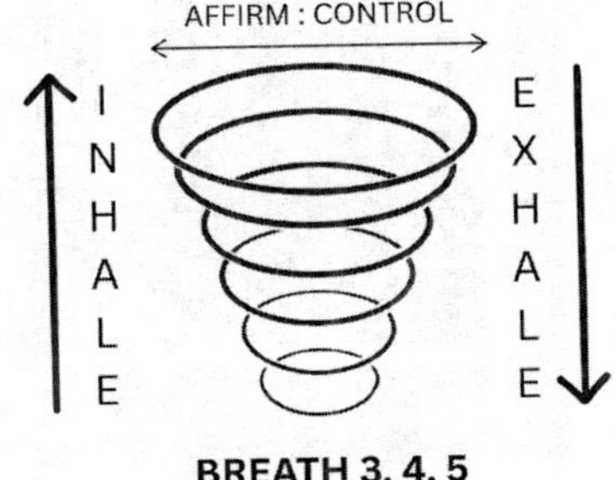

BREATH 3, 4, 5

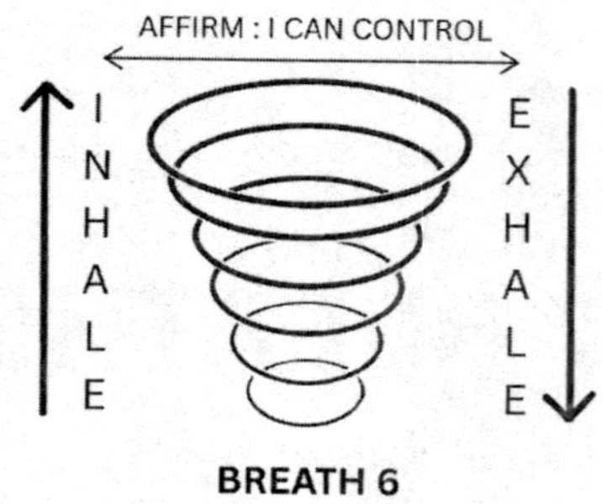

BREATH 6

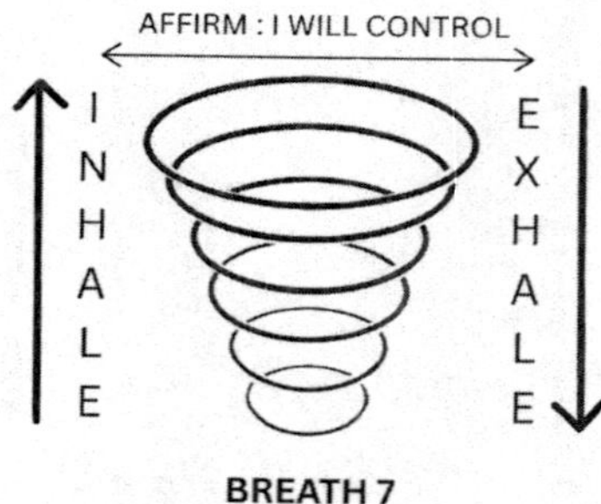

BREATH 7

Scan the QR code to begin your 7 Breaths Practice.

Follow along with a simple, guided version—your power pause before every meal.

7

The Mini Breath Reset: Three Breaths in 30 Seconds

Ever feel like seven breaths are a stretch when life gets hectic? You're not alone. During a wellness workshop that I was leading, someone asked, 'What if even seven breaths feel like too much?' That question resonated deeply with me because, honestly, I've been there too.

On those days when your mind races, your hands are full and pausing feels like a distant dream? The day often unfolds in rushed meals and unconscious snacking. Genuine hunger takes a backseat to eating prompted by stress, boredom, feeling overwhelmed or just plain autopilot. That is when the Mini Breath practice is your answer.

Just three intentional breaths—a mini pause that fits even the tightest schedules—can be powerful enough to gently steer you from craving to calm. We all have those moments when the to-do list feels endless and willpower seems to take a vacation.

The Mini Breath is the last three breaths of the 7 Breaths Practice. The Mini Breath practice is your reliable reset button for those times when minutes matter, energy is low and you simply need a moment to reconnect with yourself. It's not about striving for perfection; it's about embracing a small, consistent change that can yield significant results.

Mini Breath: Three Breaths to Reset

The Mini Breath practice draws its strength directly from breaths five, six and seven of the full 7 Breaths Practice. These final three breaths, focused on cultivating control and your commitment to it, offer remarkable power even on their own. While the full practice provides a more comprehensive grounding, the Mini Breath practice efficiently taps into this crucial element of conscious control.

Here's your quick guide:

Three affirmations. One powerful reset.

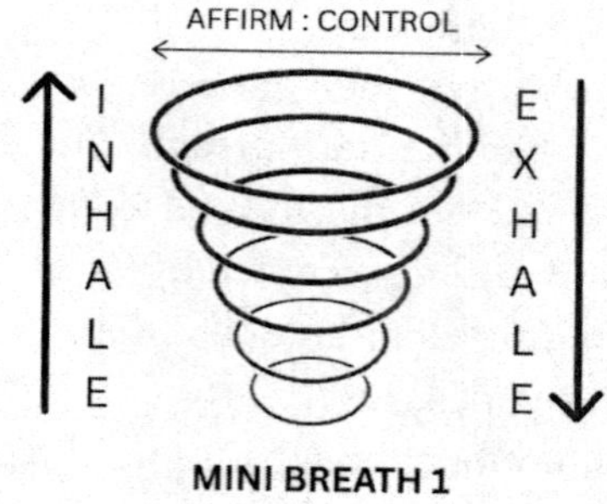

MINI BREATH 1

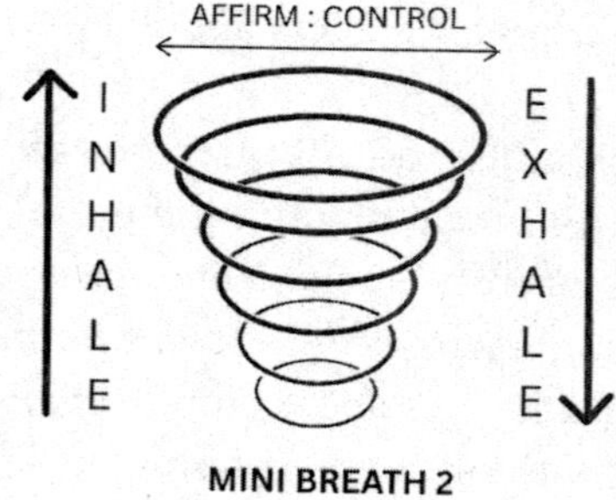

MINI BREATH 2

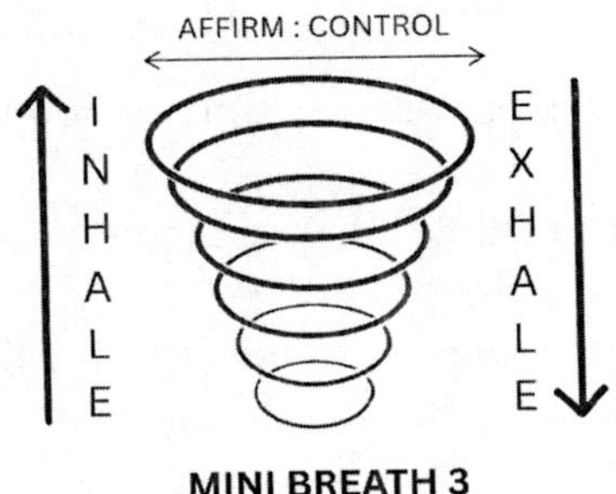

MINI BREATH 3

1. Inhale gently. Hold briefly while affirming: 'Control.' Exhale slowly.
2. Inhale again. Hold briefly while affirming: 'I can control.' Let the affirmation resonate within you. Exhale with ease.
3. Inhale deeply. Hold briefly, affirming: 'I will control.' Exhale fully.

Three breaths to go from stressed to centred—even amidst the beautiful chaos of everyday life.

Time: 30 Seconds

The Mini Breath takes about thirty seconds, though this may vary slightly depending on factors like your lung capacity, level of relaxation and personal breathing rhythm.

Key Pointers: Practise Duration and Flow

- Time: Takes approximately thirty seconds (3 breaths ≈ 30 Seconds)
- Pacing: Each breath (inhale + exhale) takes a relaxed eight to fifteen seconds.
- Guidance: No stopwatch needed. Simply listen to your body's natural rhythm for a wonderful little reset.

Why the Mini Breath Shifts Your State

Even just three slow, deep breaths have a remarkable ability to lower cortisol, calm your nervous system and sharpen your focus. When you pair this physiological response with the potent affirmations of control, you create a powerful mental shift that can interrupt a craving in its tracks.

This practice provides a vital space, that crucial gap between the initial urge and your subsequent action. It's in this space that you can consciously remember that you are in charge of your choices. This simple habit of breathing and affirming doesn't just offer temporary calm, over time, it gently rewires your thought patterns around food.

Real Moments, Real Change: The Mini Breath in Action

Many individuals who've attended my workshops or followed my guidance have embraced the Mini Breath practice and made it their own. These real-life stories illustrate the power of this simple pause in everyday situations. Remember, while each pause is brief, its cumulative effect strengthens your sense of control, leading to more consistent choices that support your goals.

- **Radhika, 45, HR Professional—Cookie Craving Reset:** 'It was 4:30 p.m., and I was about to reach for the cookie jar. Then I remembered the Mini Breath practice. The affirmations helped me pause—Control. I can control. I will control. I closed the cabinet, drank water instead and felt proud.'
- **Arjun, 21, Student—Mindless Midnight Munching:** 'I used to raid the fridge late at night. The Mini Breath practice gave me enough time to pause. Now, I have tea instead and sleep better.'
- **Neha, 38, Marketing Executive and Mom—Leftovers and Letting Go:** 'Cleaning up after my kids always led to mindless bites. Doing the Mini Breath practice before picking anything up became my new ritual. I've lost four kilos in six months and gained trust in myself.'
- **Sameer, 42, Sales Head—Travel-Time Takeback:** 'I used to skip meals and binge at airport lounges. Now, I do the Mini Breath practice before heading to the buffet. It changed my relationship with food on the road.'

Mini Breath at the Office: Your On-the-Go Slimming Tool

Next time stress hits at work, resist the urge Po grab a snack automatically. Instead, pause, take three breaths and consciously shift from reacting out of habit to responding with intention.

1. **Pre-Snack Pause in the Office Pantry:** Before reaching for that cookie or chip, do the Mini Breath practice. This helps you assess if you're truly hungry or just reacting to stress or routine.

2. **Stress Break Instead of a Snack:** Long meetings and tight deadlines can trigger stress-snacking. Instead of automatically reaching for comfort food, pause with the Mini Breath and reset your response.
3. **Breakfast Buffets during Travel:** Take the three breaths before approaching hotel buffets. You'll be more in tune with your genuine hunger cues and less likely to overindulge.
4. **Free Hampers and Lounge Buffets:** Pause before reaching for snacks in hotels or airport lounges. The three breaths help you shift from automatic munching to making focus-driven choices.
5. **At Corporate Events or Buffets:** Social events often present food temptations. Doing the Mini Breath practice before filling your plate helps you choose intentionally.
6. **Afternoon Energy Slumps:** Before reaching for sugary snacks, try the Mini Breath practice. You might realize your slimming goals are more important and opt for a smaller portion or a healthier alternative.

When to Use It: Your Pocket-Sized Pause

The Mini Breath is your readily available tool. Use it anywhere, anytime you feel that unconscious pull towards food:

- Before opening the refrigerator
- While scrolling through food delivery apps
- Standing in a takeaway or buffet line
- Before that, 'just one more bite'
- During moments of emotional or social eating

Whenever you sense yourself gravitating towards food without genuine awareness, pause. Do the Mini Breath practice.

Why This Matters: Building Your Practice for Success

The Mini Breath is a simple, repeatable practice that's quick, effective and always accessible. It empowers you to take back control.

As James Clear wisely said, 'You don't rise to the level of your goals. You fall to the level of your systems.' The Mini Breath practice is your foundational practice for conscious eating in a fast-paced world.[3]

Explore the Mini Breath practice and discover its power as an essential tool for quick resets in busy moments. It's not always meals that derail us—it's the in-between moments: stress scrolling, emotional dips, boredom, or rushed, thoughtless snacking.

Unlike the full 7 Breaths Practice, which is perfect for sitting down and tuning into a complete meal, the Mini Breath practice is a shorter, on-the-go version—quick enough to fit into the busiest schedule, yet still powerful enough to help you regain control, pause and realign with your goals. Just a few mindful inhales and exhales, and you can reset your mindset, curb impulsive eating and bring awareness back into your day.

[3]Ibid.

Real Talk

Q: Can I use the Mini Breath practice instead of the full practice?

A: Absolutely! Especially on those busy or emotionally charged days. It's far more beneficial to take those three intentional Mini Breaths than to skip the practice altogether. As you experience the positive shifts from the Mini Breath practice, you might also find yourself drawn to explore the full 7 Breaths Practice, which offers a deeper sense of calm and a more comprehensive pre-meal preparation.

Q: Will it help me slim down?

A: Yes. Slimming is about more than just the food you eat; it's deeply connected to your awareness and the trust you build in yourself. The Mini Breath practice directly supports all three of these crucial elements.

Q: Can the Mini Breath help with emotional eating too?

A: Definitely! Whether you're feeling anxious, stressed or influenced by social pressures to eat, this simple pause can provide the space you need to regain control in those challenging moments. It's about fostering awareness so you can choose your response, rather than reacting out of ingrained habit.

From Craving to Choice: Reclaiming the Moment

So much of our eating isn't driven by true hunger, but by stress, habit, or simply being distracted… The Mini Breath isn't just about resisting a snack; it's about actively reclaiming control in a world that often feels like it's moving at warp speed. It's your anchor, your quick reset and your powerful reminder that lasting change, even in your eating habits, begins with conscious discipline.

Habit Check-In: Your Mini Moment of Reflection

Take a moment to think about a situation when you typically reach for food without much thought. Ask yourself:

- What usually triggers this habit? (Stressful emails? Boredom during downtime? Watching TV?)
- What's your typical reaction? (Mindlessly snacking? Continuous grazing?)
- What are you truly seeking in that moment? (Comfort? A sense of control? Connection or distraction?)

Now, try this simple shift:

- Instead of your usual reaction, pause and do the Mini Breath practice.
- Intentionally shift your focus from the urge for food to your inner sense of self-control.
- Consider writing down one specific habit loop you'll consciously interrupt this week using the Mini Breath.

NamitaSpeaks

The Mini Breath practice is your quiet pocket of power, a gentle whisper of self-trust in a world that often feels overwhelmingly noisy. Just three conscious breaths in thirty seconds. No excuses—just three breaths to shift from cravings to calm and clear choice. It's a moment to realign, not only with your breath but with your deeper intentions. Because sustainable slimming starts not just on your plate, but in your mindset

MINI BREATH

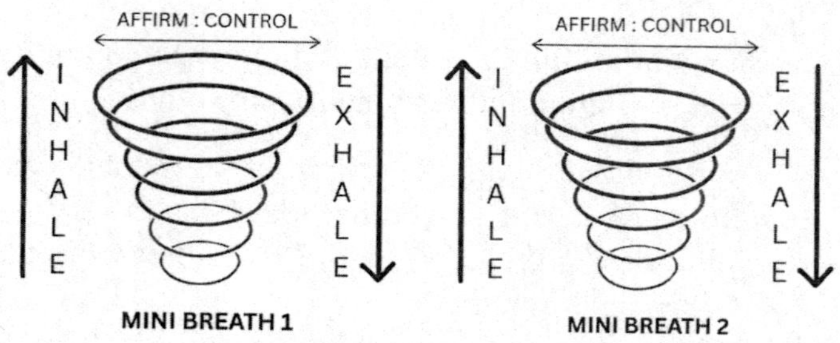

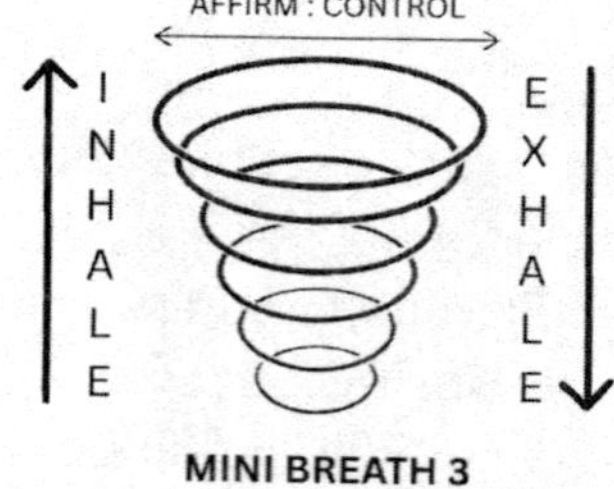

Scan the QR code to begin your Mini Breath journey. Follow along with this guided practice.

8

How Breath Shapes Your Plate: Your Empowered Eating Journey

'Mindless eating ends where mindful breathing begins.'
—Tara Brach

So true, isn't it?

Let me tell you—the 7 Breaths Practice didn't just appear out of thin air or from some dusty research paper. It grew out of my own journey, especially after I experienced weight gain.

I remember speaking at a corporate wellness seminar, sharing how something as simple as pausing to take conscious breaths before eating could truly make a difference. And then someone in the audience said something so simple, yet so profound:

'Ah…so when breath meets the plate, magic happens.'

That one sentence just clicked. It wasn't just poetic—it was the heart of it all. In that moment, I realized that something as easy and accessible as our breath, paired with a little intention, could reshape how we relate to food. This wasn't only about changing what we ate—it was about transforming how we lived.

The real magic lies in slowing down, tuning into what our bodies are telling us and gently aligning our inner selves with our slimming goals—one breath at a time.

The Core Principles of Breath-Led Eating

This simple act of pausing to breathe before eating gently reinforces three core principles—reshaping not only your plate, but also your relationship with food and your path to sustainable slimming:

- **Relaxation**: calms your nervous system, setting the stage for better digestion and more conscious choices.
- **Discipline**: builds inner control, helping you respond with intention instead of reacting impulsively.
- **Portion control**: creates a moment of awareness, guiding you to stop at 'just enough' and tune in to your body's true signals.

My Turning Point: From Rushed Meals to Real Presence

There was a time, not too long ago, when my own discipline around food started to slip. The weight was creeping up, and I felt constantly drained. Life had become this whirlwind of meetings, deadlines and those high-pressure decisions that just never seemed to end. Meals became a mechanical necessity or were skipped entirely in the chaos. I was completely disconnected from my body's signals. Eating was rushed, mindless and, way too often, driven by stress.

Then, a quiet, game-changing thought popped into my head: What if taking control wasn't about constantly saying 'no' to food, but about saying a big 'yes' to being present in the moment? That single shift changed everything.

I started experimenting with this simple pause—a little breath practice—right before I ate. No complicated calorie counting. No labelling foods as 'good' or 'bad'. I've always felt that our best food choices come from our intuition. After all, everybody is different, every metabolism is unique, and deep down, we each have this inner knowing of what truly works for us.

And just like that, 7 Breaths to Slimming was born.

A gentle, structured pause to bring my inner state into harmony with my outer actions. The impact was amazing. I started eating more slowly, actually tasting my food. I felt so much more in control (hello, discipline!). And my body? It responded with this lightness, clarity and a renewed sense of energy (reflecting better portion control and less stress). For the first time, slimming didn't feel like some kind of punishment or deprivation—it felt like freedom, like finally coming home to myself.

Joanna's Story: Change Starts with a Conscious Breath

During one of my webinars, I connected with Joanna, a brilliant and driven investment banker in the UK. Her meals were often a race against the clock—eaten hunched over her desk, squeezed between endless Zoom calls and emails. Snacking had become this automatic reflex, completely devoid of any awareness.

She started with the Mini Breath—just three slow, intentional breaths before her lunch. 'It was so easy,' she told me. 'I could do it without anyone even noticing.' Over time, she felt the shift and naturally progressed to the full 7 Breaths Practice. 'At first, it felt a little strange, to be honest. I wasn't used to pausing. But then something shifted. The breath became this cue—this moment of pure clarity before I even picked up my fork.'

That one simple pause changed everything for her. She started to notice when she was truly hungry—and, just as importantly, when she felt satisfied. She stopped eating on autopilot. Two months later, she had lost five kilos. But even more significantly, she felt this incredible sense of calm, empowerment and a deep reconnection with her body.

She called me, her voice just buzzing with excitement. 'This isn't a diet—it's a mindset,' she exclaimed. 'Can I share my story at your next webinar?'

Her journey was a powerful reminder of a simple truth: Real change doesn't require struggle—it often begins with just one conscious breath. You might wonder how this fits into busy social situations or rushed meals. The beauty lies in its adaptability. Even the thirty-second Mini Breath practice can create a crucial pause.

Remember, it's about progress, not perfection. In those faster-paced moments, the Mini Breath practice becomes your discreet and powerful tool to maintain connection and intention.

Why We Sometimes Resist the Simple Things

It's funny, isn't it? We often resist what feels new, especially when it seems too simple. But don't let simplicity fool you—it holds immense power in its quiet form. Old habits feel safe, familiar, even when they're not serving us. New habits, even the beneficial and healing ones, can feel a bit foreign and, yeah, maybe even a little uncomfortable at first.

We start telling ourselves things like: 'I'm just not in the mood right now.' Or, 'I simply don't have the time.' But let's be real, the full 7 Breaths Practice takes approximately one minute. The Mini Breath is even shorter—thirty seconds! We might even think, 'This just feels a little strange.'

Of course it does! All change feels a bit odd in the beginning. That's not a sign to stop; it's usually a sign that you're stepping into something new and positive. And then there's the classic, 'Oh, I forgot.'

That's okay! No guilt trips here. Every single meal is a fresh start, a brand new chance to come back to yourself. And if you think, 'Well, I didn't do it perfectly,' remember this isn't about some impossible standard of perfection. It's about being present in the moment. This isn't a test you can fail; it's a tool you can use.

Crucially, the 7 Breaths Practice also creates a vital space between your emotions and your eating habits. When stress, boredom or other feelings trigger the urge to eat, that pre-meal pause allows you to recognize the emotion without immediately reacting with food. It empowers you to make a conscious choice rather than an impulsive one.

You don't need to start by practising before every single meal. Just pick one to begin with. Dinner is often a great place—it tends to be a bit slower, quieter and more relaxed. Let that one moment of breath become your anchor. Then, gently, you can start to expand it to other meals. Give it a month, let it settle in, let it grow. Soon enough, it won't feel like a 'practice' anymore—it'll feel like second nature, a natural rhythm, a way of coming back to yourself.

Real People, Real Results: It Truly Works

From the workshops, retreats and webinars where I've shared the 7 Breaths to Slimming and the Mini Breath, I've heard so many stories that all point to the same encouraging truth: this simple breath practice works. Let me share a few more experiences from real people:

- *'The 7 Breaths Practice has been a game-changer for breaking my stress and emotional snacking cycles. It's honestly like flipping a switch inside me.'*—**Aarti, 34, HR professional and a busy, young mom.**
- *'I used to eat standing up, completely rushed. Now, I make a point to sit down, take a moment with the Mini Breath, and I feel so much calmer and more nourished.'*—**Richard, 48, advertising executive with a demanding schedule**
- *'Even my kids remind me now: "Mum, do your breath thing!" The way they say it sometimes, I think they might even want to join in!'*—**Neha, 28, graphic designer and a single parent**
- *'This isn't just about food for me anymore. It's about feeling more connected to myself. The 7 Breaths Practice works—I'm genuinely enjoying the whole process.'* —**Roshan, 56, retired schoolteacher, embracing a healthier chapter**

The breath isn't just a tool; it evolves into a daily practice of showing respect to your body, being present in the moment and fostering a deeper connection with yourself.

Daily Integration: Making Breath Your Ally

Let's make this tangible. Here's a glimpse into how the breath practice weaves into the daily life of Joanna, our investment banker in the UK:

- **7:30 a.m.**

  Grounded Start: Before my morning coffee or smoothie, I pause for the full 7 Breaths Practice. It helps me start my day with a sense of calm and presence.

- **1:00 p.m.**
  Midday Reset: Before lunch, I take a breath break. The 7 Breaths Practice helps me slow down and consciously choose what my body truly needs, not just what's convenient.

- **4:30 p.m.**
  Snack Pause: When those afternoon cravings hit, I reach for the Mini Breath practice— just three deep breaths. It helps me tune in and discern if it's real hunger or just a habit.

- **8:00 p.m.**
  Evening Unwind: Dinner becomes a quiet ritual. I bring in the full 7 Breaths Practice. I find that I eat slower, digest better and even sleep more soundly.

But what about those days when Joanna's completely pressed for time or juggling back-to-back tasks?

Her advice is simple and practical: *'Don't skip the practice altogether. Even when time is incredibly tight, those few breaths act as an anchor for me. I follow this flexible "breath map" to stay grounded without adding any extra pressure.'*

Notice how Joanna prioritizes consistency over rigid adherence. It's about finding what works for you in the moment, knowing that every breath you take with intention contributes to progress.

Breath before Every Bite: Joanna's Quick Day Map

- 7:00 a.m.: Mini Breath practice before morning snack
- 9:00 a.m.: Mini Breath practice before breakfast

- 12:30 p.m.: Mini Breath practice before lunch
- 4:30 p.m.: Mini Breath practice before evening snack
- 8:00 p.m.: Full 7 Breaths Practice before dinner ('Once I'm home, I'm relaxed and ready for the full practice')

NamitaSpeaks

The beauty of this practice lies in its simplicity. It's not about striving for unattainable perfection—it's about cultivating presence in each moment. Every single breath offers a chance to pause, gently reconnect with yourself and consciously shift your mindset around food. You don't have to get it 'right' every time. Just begin—exactly where you are. With time and consistency, this will start to feel natural, like a steady rhythm flowing effortlessly through your day. Let your breath be your anchor. Trust the process. The results will follow—gently, organically, with a quiet yet undeniable power. Begin your next meal or snack with a breath of awareness.

Feel the shift. Let breath shape your plate.

9

Rewire Habits with Breath

'First we make our habits, then our habits make us.'

—John Dryden

Powerful words to remember as we explore how to create lasting change.

A Jolt That Changed Everything

While working in a demanding family business, I got a jolt—a sudden realization that I had gained seven kg in just two years. It was a wake-up call.

Returning to my slimming goals couldn't stay just a vague intention. It needed to become a focused, energy-driven project. Ironically, that jolt gave me the push to regain discipline—and from there, the 7 Breaths Practice was born.

I knew I had to rebuild healthy habits, starting with portion control. That's when I developed a simple yet powerful method: 7 Breaths to Slimming. It helped me reconnect with my goals before every meal. It wasn't just a technique—it became a lifestyle shift. The real magic lay in repetition, a consistent reminder to stay focused. And yes, there were days I forgot to pause. That's okay. Progress isn't linear—it's in the return.

This practice has become a lifelong habit because real, sustainable results come from consistency, not quick fixes. And so, I'm sharing this with conviction: you can get results too. However, the key is to create your habit loop.

Office Habits: The Unseen Loop

Have you ever reached for a snack—not because you were hungry, but because it's what you always do at that hour, not as a conscious choice, but as a default? Consider those office settings where cookies and coffee are routinely served during meetings; it's easy to fall into the pattern: sip the coffee, nibble the cookie and call it a refreshing break. But is it hunger—or habit?

That's where 7 Breaths to Slimming comes in. It's not the cookie—it's the cue. The breath breaks that link. The moment before you reach for that cookie can become a cue. Not enough time to do the full practice?

Try the Mini Breath practice—a shortcut using just the last three breaths of the full 7 Breaths sequence. Mini breath works perfectly when you're in a hurry; the full 7 Breaths deepens awareness and helps reinforce long-term habits .Ask yourself: Do I truly want this, or am I just following a habit? This breath practice doesn't deprive you—it simply creates space. A pause between the craving and the consumption. Sometimes, that space is all it takes to change the choice.

From Unconscious Habit to Conscious Choice

Honestly, starting the breath technique can feel a bit like trying on a new pair of shoes— unfamiliar, maybe even a tad uncomfortable. You might find yourself forgetting to pause before eating, caught up in the momentum of your day. Doubts might even whisper in your ear, questioning its effectiveness. This is all part of the process.

Think about building any new habit. Remember the initial awkwardness of trying a new exercise routine? Your muscles protested, and your coordination felt off. But with persistence, your body adapted, grew stronger, and the movements became more natural. Similarly, learning to drive a car requires a conscious effort for every action until those actions become second nature to you.

The breath practice works in the same way—training your awareness. In the beginning, you'll need those mental post-its to remind you to pause. There will be times you forget, but with each intentional breath, you're shining a light on those unconscious habits. The pause creates space, allowing you to reflect before you react. With consistent practice, that awareness deepens.

The breath acts as your automatic reset—a mindful interruption to habitual eating. That's the beauty of the transformation: the invisible patterns of unconscious eating become visible, giving you the power to choose a new path.

A Loop That Serves You

The power of 7 Breaths to Slimming lies in repetition—and in creating a loop. A loop of awareness. A loop that serves you. Think of it like your morning tea or coffee, or those phrases you hear often in the workplace—short, familiar cues that stick over time. Just like companies reinforce values through repetition, the Breaths help you build a new rhythm before eating. It becomes comforting, predictable, and with practice, second nature.

That moment of pause can help you cut back on portions—or even skip what you don't need.

Now imagine replacing the old pattern—like reaching for a sugary snack every afternoon—with something that truly supports your goals.

A pause before action.
That moment of pause—to breathe—is the key.
Before the fork. Before the craving.
You pause. You breathe. With intention.
That's the shift. This is the new loop.

Why It Works

Old habit: Craving → Eat → Guilt
New habit: Craving → Breathe → Choose

You're no longer just reacting—you're responding with clarity. Even if the craving remains, your breath creates space. In that space, you choose to act with intention. Each breath plays a vital role in building this new loop: the first breaths help you relax, while the affirmations strengthen your focus, guiding you toward your slimming goals.

How to Rewire Your Habit Loop: Your Plan

To effectively rewire a habit, it's essential to understand its components and consciously introduce the breath practice at the right moment. Here's a simple four-step approach:

1. **Identify Your Habit Loop .** Break the habit down into its key elements:
    - Cue: What triggers your automatic eating? (Examples: feeling stressed, seeing snacks in the office, watching TV, a specific time like 4 p.m., associating meals with relaxation)

- Routine: What action do you take in response? (Examples: overeating because the food tastes good, reaching for the cookie jar, opening the fridge mindlessly, ordering takeout)
- Reward: What do you get out of the behaviour? (Examples: temporary comfort, a quick energy boost, relief from boredom, distraction)

2. **Choose Your Pause Point**: This is the moment just before the habitual action— your opportunity to pause and breathe. (Examples: before serving yourself at a buffet, opening the snack drawer, placing a food order, or taking the first bite)
3. **Insert the Breath Practice:** At your chosen pause point, practice one of the following:
   - The 7 Breaths Practice: A one-minute breathing sequence
   - The Mini Breath practice: A shorter, thirty-second version for busy moments

   The breath practice interrupts the automatic loop, reinforces your intention and creates a moment of clarity.
4. **Consciously Choose Your Response:** After your breath pause, ask yourself:
   - Am I truly hungry?
   - What does my body need right now?
   - Can I align this meal with my slimming goals?

This brief reflection allows you to shift from automatic reaction to intentional response. You might choose to:

- Eat with portion awareness
- Opt for a lighter option
- Eat less—or simply wait until later if you're not hungry

Real-Life in Action: Rewiring the Evening Habits

Meet Rita—a working mom who realized she was snacking every evening while watching TV. It wasn't true hunger, just a reflex at the end of a long day.

Here's how she applied the four-step process:

- Cue: Turning on the TV after dinner
- Routine: Grabbing chips or cookies
- Reward: A sense of comfort and unwinding

Rita chose her pause point just before heading to the kitchen. Instead of reaching for snacks, she practised the 7 Breaths Practice. After the pause, she asked herself, 'Am I truly hungry? What does my body need?'

She swapped the snacks for a soothing cup of tea—not as a punishment, but as a new way to care for herself. In that pause, she discovered something more satisfying than the crunch: a sense of calm and control.

With each evening, the craving grew quieter and her confidence grew stronger. Real change didn't happen in a single moment—it happened in the rhythm she repeated.

Real-Life in Action: Rewiring the Dinner-Indulgence Habit

Meet Arjun—a mid-level corporate executive who often worked long hours. By the time he got home, he was mentally drained and emotionally spent. Dinner became his reward not just a meal but a ritual of indulgence to soothe the day's stress.

Here's how he applied the four-step process:

- Cue: Logging off his laptop around 9 p.m., feeling mentally exhausted

- Routine: Ordering takeout or binge-eating a heavy dinner in front of his phone
- Reward: A sense of relief, comfort and escape

Arjun's turning point came when he noticed how sluggish and bloated he felt the next morning. He chose his pause point right after shutting down his computer. Instead of heading straight to the kitchen, he practised the 7 Breaths Practice.

After that short pause, he asked himself: '*Is this heavy food what I need—or just a break from stress? Can I find comfort in a way that supports my health?*'

He began replacing indulgent meals with lighter options and smaller portions—eating just enough to feel nourished, not stuffed. He also added a short evening walk or calming music as a more genuine way to unwind.

Slowly, the cycle shifted—from numbing stress with food to processing it and restoring his energy. With consistency, Arjun's evenings transformed. He no longer overate to escape—he ate to nourish and honour his body's needs.

Two Stories, One Powerful Shift

Whether it's Rita reaching for snacks while watching TV or Arjun winding down with an oversized dinner after work, both stories reveal how easily comfort can become a cue for unconscious eating. But with a single pause—just a few intentional breaths—the loop can be gently interrupted and rewired.

The shift doesn't begin with force or restriction, but with awareness. With each breath, a new pattern takes root: Less reacting. More choosing.

Try it for just one week. Commit to one habit, one pause, with breath practice—and let that be the start of lasting change. Because real change doesn't come in a dramatic moment—it comes in the rhythm you repeat.

Real Change Begins in Repetition

Repetition isn't boring. It's the rhythm of transformation.

7 Breaths to Slimming isn't a one-time fix. It's a rhythm you return to, again and again, until it becomes part of who you are. Think about it: in the corporate world, progress comes from consistent habits, not one-off brilliance.

In fitness, showing up regularly matters more than the occasional perfect workout. Small, steady efforts beat sporadic bursts of intensity. And in spiritual traditions, repetition is sacred. From chanting the *Gayatri Mantra* or *Mahamrityunjaya Mantra* in Hinduism (prayers for wisdom and protection), to reciting the rosary in Christianity (meditative repetition of prayers), *dhikr* in Islam (remembrance of God through repeated phrases), *Nam Myōhō Renge Kyō* in Nichiren Buddhism (affirming devotion to the Mystic Law of the Lotus Sutra), or sutras in Zen practice (scriptural chanting), each repeated phrase becomes more than sound—it becomes a focus, a rhythm and a tool for grounding the mind.

Repetition, when paired with earnest belief, transforms simple practice into profound change. Each act becomes charged with intention, and over time, consistency turns belief into embodied habit and lasting transformation.

Each breath, each pause, each word is an imprint on the subconscious. A pattern of devotion. A rhythm that transforms.

Over time, what begins as a simple breath practice evolves into a powerful inner shift.

The essence of this book lies in embracing the power of consistent, intentional breath practice that transforms your relationship with food and your identity. No pressure to be perfect—just the power of returning.

Real change doesn't happen in a single moment. It happens in a thousand quiet ones. Each breath is a small act of becoming. Each pause is a return to presence. Each repetition is a quiet rewire. This is how identity is formed—not in intensity, but in consistency.

Who You Are Becoming

Every time you pause, even for a moment, you're casting a vote for the kind of person you want to be. James Clear, author of *Atomic Habits*, says it best: 'Every action you take is a vote for the type of person you wish to become.' With each breath, you're not just delaying a craving—you're affirming your identity. You're telling yourself: I am someone who pauses.

I am someone who chooses with intention. I am someone who cares for my well-being and works towards my goals. Consistent practice shapes your identity as someone who is in control of their choices and committed to their health. This journey isn't about perfection; it's about progress and direction.

Habits in Real Life

The world's most successful people aren't just defined by talent—they're shaped by the small, consistent habits they commit to daily.

- Serena Williams, tennis legend, honed her craft through disciplined repetition, practising her serve for hours daily. Like the 7 Breaths, her mastery came from consistent effort.

- Warren Buffett, billionaire investor, spends up to eighty per cent of his day reading and reflecting. His success is rooted in the quiet, daily habit of a thoughtful pause, similar to the breath.
- P.V. Sindhu, Olympic badminton medallist, starts her day at 4 a.m. daily. This ritual gives her clarity and control.
- Michelle Obama, former First Lady, despite her demanding schedule, carved out time for fitness daily—showing that health isn't a luxury; it's a non-negotiable.
- Jocko Willink, retired Navy SEAL, wakes up at 4:30 a.m. daily. His photos of his watch are a reminder: consistency is strength.

Each of them proves: success isn't spontaneous. It's built on steady, repeatable actions. Just like this breath practice. Just like your new habit loop.

NamitaSpeaks

You don't need drastic overhauls. What you need is something simple, sustainable and easy to practise—like pausing meals, snacks or moments of stress. Choose the one-minute 7 Breaths Practice or the quick 30-second Mini Breath practice—the key is making it a habit loop: a consistent pause that becomes your automatic response. What matters most is doing it regularly. Progress, not perfection, drives lasting change.

10

Breathwork Journal: Your Roadmap to Real Results

'Awareness is the first step in transformation'
—Robin Sharma

This simple truth lies at the heart of why journalling can be a powerful ally on your slimming journey. While it's tempting to seek external fixes—new diets, apps, quick hacks—the real key lies within your thoughts and feelings.

Journalling changes not just what's on your plate, but how you relate to food, and how you think, feel, and eat. Ask yourself: Are you eating to satisfy genuine hunger, or are you driven by ingrained habit?

Most people understandably focus on what they eat when trying to slim down. But the real, lasting shift happens when you also pay attention to how you eat—and how much.

That's why the powerful synergy between 7 Breaths to Slimming and consistent journalling creates profound and sustainable change.

This isn't about tedious calorie counting or restrictive rules. It's about cultivating self-reflection, gaining better portion control and building unwavering consistency in your steady and thoughtful approach to food.

Your journal becomes a personal compass—capturing not just what you eat, but how you feel when you pause, and, more importantly, how your breath practice is transforming your habits.

The Undeniable Power of Tracking

Tracking is often seen as a business tool, but its impact on personal well-being is just as powerful.

Take my cousin, for example—a remarkably successful business tycoon who manages to stay incredibly fit despite a schedule that would make most of our heads spin. His secret? He diligently tracks his meals, workouts and even his sleep every single day in a simple handwritten journal—complete with little stars for days he stays on track and honest notes when he slips.

That same discipline and attention to detail that builds business empires can also shape your health and well-being. The truth is, consistent journalling drives tangible results.

Discipline born of awareness, not impulse. Each pause for breath practice before a meal creates a moment of intention. Writing it down strengthens this habit and deepens the link between breath, awareness and the way you approach food.

Take a moment to reflect and jot down your thoughts:

- Did I consciously practise the 7 Breaths or the Mini Breath before I started eating this meal? Why or why not?
- When I felt the urge for that snack, did I intentionally pause with the breath practice before reaching for it? What was I feeling in that moment?
- When you actively track your behaviours and intentions,

you move beyond mere guesswork and step firmly onto the path of real, lasting transformation.

Setting up Your Breathwork Journal: Your Meal-by-Meal Log

This journal is your guide, a space to track not just what you eat, but how you feel, when you pause, and how your breath practice is helping shift your habits.

To make your journal a true roadmap, use a consistent format. Log each meal or snack, with special attention to your breath practice before eating. This structure helps you capture the essential details that reveal your patterns and progress over time.

Here's a simple framework to get you started:

Log for each meal or snack:

- Time and meal (e.g., '1:00 p.m.—lunch')
- Hunger level before breath practice (1 = starving, 10 = stuffed)
- Breath practice used (7 Breaths/Mini Breath/Skipped)
- How I felt during the pause (e.g., 'calm', 'stressed', 'craving sugar', 'peaceful')
- Hunger level after Breath (notice if it shifted—even slightly)
- What I ate (simple description—no calorie counting needed)
- Fullness level after eating (1–10; aim to stop around 7–8—about eighty per cent full)
- Triggers or emotions (e.g., 'bored', 'tired', 'social gathering', 'rewarded myself')
- Insight or goal for next meal (e.g., 'ate slowly', 'will drink water first', 'felt proud I paused')

Why It Works

This simple act of logging helps you see the direct impact of your breath practice on your eating decisions and emotional state. It turns abstract awareness into visible patterns—and that's where real change begins.

Start Simple, Grow Strong: A Gradual Four-Week Plan

If the idea of incorporating the 7 Breaths before every single meal feels a little overwhelming right now, that's perfectly okay. As you begin to integrate the 7 Breaths or the Mini Breath practice into more of your eating occasions, here's a gentle way to build your journalling habit alongside it:

- Week 1: Begin with dinner—often the meal where you have a little more time and feel more relaxed. Commit to journalling this one meal daily, noting your breath practice and eating experience.
- Week 2: Add lunch. Now journal both lunch and dinner, observing the differences in your approach and how you feel before and after each meal.
- Week 3: Extend the practice to breakfast. This sets an intentional tone for your entire day. Aim to consistently journal all three main meals.
- Week 4: Add snacks. By now, the act of pausing before eating will likely feel more natural, almost second nature. Log your breath practice and observations for all snacks throughout the day.

By the time you reach week four, you may find that making conscious choices about portions and timing feels intuitive.

And your journal? It becomes a tangible, empowering reflection of your transformation—one breath, one meal at a time.

The breath practice: you have two options to choose from—the full 7 Breaths Practice and the Mini Breath practice, depending on what you need in the moment.

The Mini Breath practice is a quick reset—perfect for times when the urge to eat isn't about physical hunger but comes from stress, boredom or emotional triggers. It's essentially the last three breaths of the full 7 Breaths Practice.

The 7 Breaths Practice offers a complete, grounding pause to centre you before any meal.

Both tools are here to support you—use whichever feels right for you at the time.

Real-Life Success Stories: Transforming Habits

The journey to slimming often begins with a shift in awareness. 7 Breaths to Slimming—a practice I developed—helped Joe, Asha and Meera build a healthier relationship with food. It gave them the clarity and pause they needed to change long-standing habits. Here's how this simple practice became a turning point in their transformation.

Joe's Journey—From Speed Eater to Strategic Diner: Joe Samuel, 40, a marketing executive, used to rush through dinner on autopilot. After trying the 7 Breaths Practice during a corporate workshop, he had a breakthrough just days into journalling: he wasn't hungry—he was eating out of habit. By pausing before meals, his portions naturally shrank, and his stubborn paunch started to disappear. 'I didn't drastically change what I ate—just how I approached food,' Joe says. That shift turned him from a distracted eater into a careful one.

Asha's Strategy—From Emotional Eating to Empowering Rituals: Asha Taneja, 38, a college professor, reached for snacks to cope with stress. She came across the 7 Breaths Practice during a workshop at her college and decided to give it a try. Journalling the breathwork helped her recognize this emotional trigger. She began replacing snacks with calming walks and found clarity by recording her emotions in her journal. Her evening routine evolved into an empowering ritual—not a reaction to stress, but a step towards health.

Meera Iyer's Comeback—From New Mom Fatigue to Renewed Energy: New mom Meera struggled with exhaustion and mindless snacking. Discovering the 7 Breaths Practice through an online support group, she began journalling and practising a brief pause before meals. In just a few weeks, she was eating less, feeling more energized and regaining control. The breath practice made all the difference.

Why Journalling Works

The Science Speaks. The power of journalling isn't just anecdotal; numerous studies back it up. A landmark study conducted by Kaiser Permanente's Centre for Health Research followed over 1,600 participants in a dedicated weight-loss programme. The findings were truly striking: those individuals who consistently kept daily food journals experienced twice as much weight loss compared to those who didn't track their intake.[4]

---

[4]J.F. Hollis, Gullion, C.M., Stevens, V.J., Brantley, P.J., Appel, L.J., Ard, J.D., & Weight Loss Maintenance Trial Research Group (2008), Weight loss during the intensive intervention phase of the weight-loss maintenance trial, *American Journal of Preventive Medicine*, 35(2), pp. 118–126.

Consistent tracking builds profound self-awareness, and heightened awareness is the catalyst that drives lasting behavioural change. A study in the journal *Appetite* found that journalling meals and emotions helped reduce binge eating and fostered a healthier relationship with food.[5] Simply observing habits with curiosity, not judgement, led to more intentional choices.

That's the true power of journalling. It slows you down, brings automatic habits into conscious awareness and strengthens the link between intention and action. When combined with 7 Breaths to Slimming, it creates a powerful synergy, helping you stay in control, especially in moments when impulse might otherwise take over.

Your Daily Checklist for Conscious Eating

To support and deepen your journalling practice, consider reflecting on these key questions each day:

- Did I pause for seven breaths before this meal? If not, what got in the way?
- Did I use the Mini Breath practice during moments of stress or rushing?
- How did I feel—physically and emotionally—before and after eating? Were there any noticeable shifts?
- Did I stop eating when I felt about eighty per cent full?
- What patterns or triggers surfaced today around food? What may have triggered them?
- What step can I take tomorrow to move forward with greater awareness?

---

[5]Consistent food journalling can double weight loss in clinical settings by increasing self-awareness, a finding established in studies like the one by Kaiser Permanente's CHR (Hollis et al., 2008).

Let these reflections be gentle nudges—daily anchors guiding you towards deeper insight and lasting change.

NamitaSpeaks

Motivation is fleeting. True and lasting commitment, on the other hand, is something you actively design and cultivate. The breath practice gives you the essential tool of control. Your journal brings clarity over time. Together, this powerful combination reshapes your relationship with food through empowered self-awareness.

Even tuning in during your meal to notice when you're nearing eighty per cent fullness can be a gentle yet powerful shift. Track it diligently. Truly understand it. And you will see the slimming results you desire.

Every breath, every note in your journal, is a step toward the empowered, intuitive eater you're becoming. Stay consistent, and the results will follow.

SECTION THREE

The Result-Oriented Path: The Journey to Slimming Success

You've learned to breathe, to pause and to find stillness within the whirlwind. Now, it's time to translate that powerful inner work into tangible results. In this section, we'll dive into the practical, real-world applications of 7 Breaths to Slimming. We'll strip away the confusion of endless diets and tackle the most common challenges that derail even the best intentions.

From understanding the quiet wisdom of your weighing scale to developing healthy habits in the corporate jungle or at your favourite restaurant—and even uncovering the sneaky traps in 'healthy' foods—you'll discover how small, intentional shifts, anchored by your breath, can lead to visible, sustainable change.

Let this be a time to align your inner clarity with progress that flows naturally.

1

The Weighing Scale and Why It Matters

'What gets measured, gets managed.'

—Peter Drucker

The Day My Jeans Were Snug

Ever had that moment when your clothes speak louder than your reflection? I did. My favourite jeans refused to button, and the scale confirmed what I'd been ignoring.

I had immersed myself in wellness for years—authoring books, writing fitness columns, conducting workshops, mentoring beauty pageants and consulting at a leading hospital. Discipline wasn't just a habit; it was who I was.

Then life shifted. A whirlwind phase in our family business swept me up—travel, meetings, and endless hours. Meals became rushed. Workouts faded. Slowly, wellness drifted to the background.

One morning, my favourite jeans fit too snug. It was a quiet, jarring moment; a truth I could no longer overlook. I stepped on the scale. The number didn't lie. More than the weight, it reflected my disconnection from myself.

That was the moment I realigned. Not from guilt, but from clarity. I developed a technique I resonate with—7 Breaths to Slimming—to gently reset my habits. This gentle practice of seven conscious breaths became intertwined with my daily check-in on the scale, fostering a sense of calm intention. And I began weighing myself daily. Not with dread, but with intention. At first, I feared the scale. But over time, I discovered its quiet wisdom. It became a mirror, not of vanity, but of truth.

A Gentle Note before You Begin

Daily weigh-ins are a helpful tool for many, but they may not be for everyone. If you've struggled with disordered eating or body image issues, this approach might feel triggering. Your journey is yours to shape with kindness, not pressure. Always prioritize mental and emotional well-being as you pursue physical health. If the thought of daily weigh-ins brings up anxiety, consider taking a few slow, deliberate breaths before stepping on the scale to ground yourself.

Why the Number Matters (Even If You Pretend It Doesn't): Many people shy away from the scale, dreading the number that might appear: 'What if I've gained?' (Cue internal panic, as if a few grams from that surprisingly good office birthday cake might derail the cosmos.)

But here's the truth: research shows that regular weigh-ins help you stay on track. A study found that daily self-weighing encourages accountability and supports lasting behavioural change.[6]

When you face the number—yes, even when it's not your favourite—you gain insight. And insight is power. That quiet confrontation with reality can nudge you toward smarter choices (like maybe skipping a second slice… or artfully

---

[6]Madigan, C.D., et al., 'Is Self-Weighing an Effective Tool for Weight Loss: A Systematic Literature Review and Meta-Analysis', *International Journal of Behavioral Nutrition and Physical Activity*, Vol. 12, 2015, https://tinyurl.com/3tb7duu4. Accessed on 1 December 2025.

dodging cake indulgence altogether).

Awareness is the first spark of transformation. Or at the very least, the spark for a slightly more disciplined tomorrow.

The Slow Rise of Weight Gain We all know the feeling—your shirt tugs a little, your jeans won't zip quite right, or a general sluggishness sets in. Weight gain doesn't roar in like a storm—it creeps in with quiet footsteps. A few skipped workouts. A late-night dessert. A celebratory dinner. A stressful week. Daily weigh-ins act as gentle checkpoints, helping you catch small shifts before they become big problems—or a full-blown wardrobe crisis. As the old saying goes: 'A stitch in time saves nine'—and regular weigh-ins might just save your wardrobe.

The Scale: Reflection, Not Judgement

When I spoke to people on their slimming journey about weighing themselves daily, many were reluctant at first. They associated the scale with guilt, pressure, or even failure (as if that digital display holds the key to your entire self-worth—spoiler alert: it doesn't, but it does know your weight).

Yet, with a small shift in mindset, something began to change. The scale became less of a judge and more of a quiet mirror. Some found that taking a few of the 7 breaths before stepping on helped them approach the number with calm, curiosity, and less judgement.

Real stories echo this transformation:

- James, a venture capitalist, avoided the scale for six months during intense work travel. 'When I finally did, I had gained 7 kilos,' he shared. 'Had I stayed connected, I would've caught it earlier.'

- Ravi, adapting to a high-stress job in a chaotic city, realized too late that his go-to T-shirts were snug. His wake-up call wasn't dramatic—it was honest.
- Ananya, planning her wedding, avoided the scale until her dream blouse didn't fit. Instead of spiralling, she reframed the ritual. She began checking in daily, not from fear, but with calm intention. Paired with the 7 Breaths Practice she had learned, her weigh-in became a moment of presence and self-care rather than anxiety.

These aren't tales of failure. They're stories of realignment.

But what about fluctuations? Should you weigh yourself when your weight fluctuates? The answer is yes—but with a thoughtful approach. Daily weight changes are normal and often influenced by factors other than fat gain such as:

- Water retention
- Hormonal shifts (especially around your menstrual cycle)
- High salt intake
- Certain medications (like steroids or antidepressants)
- Variations in sleep or digestion

Weighing yourself regularly is helpful—but it's important to see the bigger picture. Not every uptick on the scale means you're gaining fat. When the number is higher than expected, take a moment to breathe and remind yourself that fluctuations are natural and don't signal failure. View the scale as a source of information, not judgement.

If you notice a consistent or significant change over time, it's wise to pause and reflect on what might be causing it. Let your weighing routine be guided by curiosity and self-kindness, not stress. Choose habits that leave you feeling informed, empowered, and calm.

When Experts Say 'Don't Weigh Yourself Daily'

Many dieticians and wellness experts caution against daily weigh-ins. They argue it can lead to obsession or discouragement and that your weight shouldn't define your self-worth. And yes, self-worth is not a number. But let's not confuse self-worth with self-awareness.

If we're on a slimming journey, isn't it natural—and necessary—to track progress? Would you set off on a road trip without checking the map, or ignore your fuel gauge and hope you'll arrive?

The scale, when used with intention, not obsession, isn't a judge. It's a guide.

Beyond the Number: Why Your Weight Is Just Part of the Story

The number on the scale gets all the attention, but your body is a complex, dynamic system. What really matters is what your weight is made of—fat, muscle, water—and how these pieces shape your health and vitality. Let's dig deeper into what your scale can tell you… and what it can't.

What the Scale Really Tells You

Weight alone doesn't tell the full story. What truly matters is your body composition—the balance between:

- Fat vs. Muscle
- Fat: especially visceral fat, surrounds internal organs and poses health risks.
- Muscle: your metabolism booster, strength builder and posture protector.

Types of Fat

- Subcutaneous fat: the soft layer just beneath your skin.
- Visceral fat: deep abdominal fat—less visible but more dangerous.

Practising 7 Breaths regularly can boost your body awareness, helping you notice subtle shifts in energy and how different foods affect you—insights that go beyond the number on the scale.

Smart Ways to Track Fat Loss (Without a Smart Scale)

1. Waist Circumference
    - Women: Aim for under thirty-five inches
    - Men: Aim for under forty inches
2. Waist-to-Hip Ratio
    - Healthy range: Women under 0.85 | men under 0.90
3. Body Mass Index (BMI)
    - 18.5–24.9 is considered normal (though not always ideal for muscular builds)
4. Body Composition Analysis (BCA)
    - Use smart scales or gym devices to measure body fat per cent, muscle mass and more

Embracing Tech, Taking Perspective

Modern smart scales sync with your phone and track:

- Body fat percentage
- Muscle and bone mass
- Water content

Don't get thrown off by daily fluctuations—hydration, salt intake and hormones all influence the numbers. Focus on trends, not daily spikes.

Do You Know? The Scale's Surprising Origins

Did you know weighing scales date back to around 2000 BCE? The earliest versions were balance scales used in Egypt to measure gold and grains. Fast forward to today, and we have smart scales that can analyse your muscle mass, hydration levels and even metabolic age—all while syncing to your phone! From measuring sacks of wheat to decoding body composition, the humble scale has truly evolved.

The Scale as an Accountability Partner

Change the narrative: The scale isn't your opponent—it's your accountability partner.

- One day up? That's okay.
- Two days up? Pause and reflect.
- Three days up? Time to gently reassess.

Let that check-in be rooted in self-respect, not judgement.

A Daily Ritual for Clarity

Try this simple morning practice:

1. Wake up.
2. Use the bathroom.
3. Take slow, gentle breaths to centre yourself.
4. Step on the scale.

5. Log the number.
6. Smile, breathe and move on.

It's not about obsessing—it's about caring.

Interesting Insight: Pilots, Astronauts and... You?

Even NASA astronauts and airline pilots are required to monitor their weight regularly—not for looks, but for performance and safety.

In space, body weight affects bone density, muscle mass and mission success. On Earth, pilots monitor it to ensure aircraft balance.

The takeaway? Weight isn't about vanity—it's about function, awareness and control. Just like them, you're navigating important terrain: your health.

So, the next time you step on the scale, remember—you're not obsessing. You're operating your mission control.

NamitaSpeaks

Let the scale be your companion, not your critic. A number does not define you, but you can be guided by it. With curiosity, compassion and courage, embrace the scale as a partner on your wellness journey. Let it bring you closer to your slimming goals—and your most vibrant self.

2

7 Habits That Work

Slim down, Power up

What if slimming down didn't drain your energy, but actually supercharged it? You know that feeling—finally zipping up your favourite jeans and suddenly being filled with a surge of energy. It's not just about the fit; it's that newfound confidence unlocking a hidden feistiness. You step out ready to take on the day, and your inner voice—usually hesitant—feels bolder and more in charge. You're not just someone who fits into their jeans; you're a force to be reckoned with, armed with a trimmer waistline and fresh empowerment. It's the quiet confidence that comes with a mission accomplished—you did it, and now you own it.

7 Breaths to Slimming isn't just a method—it's the anchor for your transformation. Think of it as your personal life raft in the never-ending ocean of weight-loss advice.

Whether you're leading board meetings, managing a household, or balancing both, this approach meets you where you are on your slimming journey. If you crave structure, results and simplicity, this plan is for you. You don't need to overhaul your life, just fit a smarter system into it. This approach is practical, doable and designed to keep you centred through the chaos. Small, intentional actions—done consistently—lead to real change. No guilt. No extremes. Just a more sustainable way to take charge of your energy, your goals and your slimming results.

African Proverb: A cat that dreams of becoming a lion must lose its appetite for rats.

To achieve something extraordinary, you must let go of habits that no longer serve your higher self. If slimming is your goal, it's time to release what's holding you back—mindless snacking while scrolling through endless social media, skipping meals with the classic 'I'm too busy' excuse, playing the blame game and that ever-familiar loop of self-judgement.

It's time to trade those patterns for habits that align with your vision—and the more focused version of you.

Now that you've understood the breath practice, it's time to activate it for real-world slimming results. The essence of 7 Breaths to Slimming is discipline, not deprivation. It's about portion control and daily routines that support your weight-loss goals.

These seven steps make slimming practical, sustainable and empowering. You hold the power to choose what goes on your plate. Since your lifestyle habits, food preferences and metabolism are unique, your approach should be too. You've likely tried a few diets already, and you know what resonates and what doesn't. Let this be your reminder: sustainable change begins with intention, grows with awareness and thrives when you honour what truly works for you.

Amid meetings, deadlines and decision fatigue, slimming down doesn't need to add stress, it can become your anchor.

These are your 7 real-life slimming habits—rooted in breath, powered by intention.

When I was recently invited to speak at a prestigious

club event attended by professionals, entrepreneurs and wellness enthusiasts, the topic of my talk was '7 Breaths to Slimming—A Sustainable Approach to Weight Loss'. The response was overwhelmingly positive. People came up to me and said, 'This finally makes sense!' and 'I feel like I can do this'.

Rooted in breath, awareness and intention, the essence of that talk is presented to you in this chapter. After the session, many attendees began applying these tools and shared their success stories with me. Their journeys—drawn from everyday life—prove that meaningful change is possible, even with packed schedules.

Turn Your Breath Practice into Real Slimming Results.

Here are 7 steps to show how you can begin turning your breath practice into real, tangible results:

1. **Weigh Daily—Own Your Journey**
   Action Step: Every morning, step on the scale. Note the number—no judgement, just observation.
   Why It Works: Daily tracking builds awareness and sets a purposeful tone for your day. Much like your breath practice cultivates focused attention, this simple ritual grounds you in the present and keeps your slimming journey intentional.
   Real-Life Success: Akhil Shukla, 36, a tech CEO, began weighing himself each morning. This one step built accountability and kept him focused. Over six months, Akhil shed 5 stubborn kilos and now maintains his weight. 'I don't let a week slip by—I know where I stand

each morning.'

2. **Plan Your Meals—Like You Organize Your Day**
   Action Step: Plan your meals like you plan your meetings—structured and intentional.
   Why It Works: When meals are part of your daily plan, they stop being afterthoughts and start aligning with your goals. The intentionality you bring to meal planning mirrors the conscious pause in your breath practice—helping you make deliberate, empowered choices instead of impulsive ones.
   Real-Life Success: Anna, 41, a full-time working mother of three, struggled with inconsistent eating. On Sundays, she began planning her meals—groceries, snacks, and weekday bites. In three months, she felt lighter, more energetic and empowered. 'Meal planning was the anchor I didn't know I needed,' she exclaimed.
3. **Pre-Meal Breathing—Anchor Your Energy**
   Action Step: Before meals or snacks, practise the full 7 Breaths sequence—or, when short on time, use the Mini Breath practice (the last 3 breaths of the practice). Even this shorter version creates a valuable pause before eating.
   Why It Works: This simple pause reconnects you to your body and your goals, helping to break the cycle of mindless eating—you know, that moment when half the chips packet is gone and you barely remember eating any. By calming the mind and enhancing interoceptive awareness, this practice helps you tune in to when you're truly hungry and how much you actually need to eat, so you make more intentional choices.
   Real-Life Success: Raj, 45, a senior lawyer, adopted the

7 Breaths Practice before lunch and dinner and the Mini Breath before snacks. This calming ritual helped him tune in to hunger and eat with control. Raj gushed, 'I went shopping for fitted T-shirts—to flaunt my belly!'

4. **The Power of No—Resist the Temptation**
   Action Step: Practise saying 'no' to second helpings or food temptations, even when others encourage you to eat more. It's okay to politely decline without guilt. You're not hurting their feelings; you're honouring your waistline.
   Why It Works: Saying 'no' strengthens your self-discipline and reinforces your commitment to your goals. It teaches you to listen to your body, not social pressure. The inner calm fostered by your breath practice can provide the steady resolve needed to politely decline temptations, allowing you to listen to your body's wisdom over external pressures.
   Real-Life Success: Sonia, 29, a senior advertising manager, found it difficult to resist tempting offers from friends and family. Once she began saying 'no' to second servings, she reduced unnecessary calorie intake. 'Saying no feels empowering!' She affirmed.
5. **Identify Stress Triggers—Stay One Step ahead**
   Action Step: Know what throws you off. Stay hydrated, keep healthy snacks and manage stress with movement or meditation or just a really good dance session.
   Why It Works: Preparedness helps you avoid reactive eating and stay intentional. Just as 7 Breaths brings calm amidst stress, proactively managing triggers helps you navigate challenges with greater awareness and less reactive eating.
   Real-Life Success: Neha, 33, an event planner, used to reach for sugar and chips during stress. Once she identified her

triggers—dehydration, sleep deprivation constant travel—she carried almonds and protein bars and did the Mini Breath practice. In Neha's words, 'Once I became aware, I wasn't helpless anymore.'

6. **Reset Quickly—No Guilt, Just Shift**

   Action Step: Slip-ups happen. Pause. Immediately engage in a slow, calming breath to interrupt feelings of guilt or failure. Then return to your full breath practice and make a fresh start.

   Why It Works: Quick recovery keeps you on track and prevents the guilt spiral. Returning to your breath practice after a slip-up acts as an anchor, helping you release guilt and gently refocus on your goals with renewed calm.

   Real-Life Success: Gaurav, 48, a senior executive, used to feel like he'd 'ruined' a day after overeating. Learning the reset mindset helped him shift perspective. 'I don't wait for Monday to start again,' he explained. The breath practice and a smart breakfast helped him feel in charge, without punishment.

7. **Journal Your Journey—Reflect and Rewire**

   Action Step: Each night, write:

   - What went well
   - What you learned
   - How your breath helped
   - One thing to improve tomorrow

   Why It Works: Journalling builds self-awareness, reveals patterns and strengthens emotional clarity. Reflecting on how your breath practice supported your day further strengthens the mind-body connection, reinforcing its role in your overall well-being and slimming efforts.

   Real-Life Success: Sarah, 43, a homemaker and mom, found journalling revealed how emotions influenced her food choices. 'Now I write it down—and reflect instead. Sometimes I even write a strongly worded letter to my cravings,' she remarked with a grin. She saw clear patterns, made intentional changes and slimmed down with portion control.

Troubleshooting Your Breath Practice

- Forgetting? Set gentle reminders on your phone or anchor the practice to an existing routine (e.g., before sitting down to eat).
- Feeling rushed? Even a few conscious breaths are better than none. The Mini Breath practice is your ally here.
- Feeling self-conscious? You can make your breathing subtle and internal. The benefit is for you.
- Noticing immediate effects? Be patient. Like any habit, the benefits of consistent breathwork build over time.

Making These Habits Work in Busy Lives

These steps may seem small, but when practised consistently, they create lasting change. They're especially effective for people who thrive on structure—checklists, schedules and clear goals. Once integrated, these habits become second nature.

I've seen CEOs, lawyers, planners, mothers and entrepreneurs thrive using this rhythm. They don't have hours to spend at the gym, but they do seek simplicity and self-mastery. And that's exactly what these steps deliver: clarity, consistency, and control—without the chaos.

What You Can Do Today

If you want to slim down but can't bear the thought of strict diets or complex routines, try these steps. They don't demand more time—just more intention.

- Weigh yourself daily.
- Plan your meals.
- Do the breath practice before meals.
- Say NO to temptation.
- Identify your stress triggers and prepare for them.
- Reset if you slip—without guilt.
- Journal your breath practice.

It's not about being perfect—it's about showing up. With breath, awareness and clear focus. The rest will follow. As one participant told me: 'I finally feel like I have a system that works with my life, not against it.' And that's what slimming success is truly about.

NamitaSpeaks

Remember these seven steps. They are your micro-victories. Each breath you take, each pause before a meal, with each intentional choice, you're building momentum.

These small actions add up. They create real, lasting change. They empower you on your slimming journey—and keep you focused and grounded through even your busiest days.

3

Corporate Eating—Navigating Office Traps

'In the midst of movement and chaos, keep stillness inside of you.'

—Deepak Chopra

Welcome to the real world of jam-packed calendars, tight deadlines and meetings, powered by caffeine and urgency—where food often becomes an afterthought, an escape, or a reward. Because who hasn't devoured an entire packet of biscuits during a particularly gruelling budget review?

The Corporate Eating Conundrum: Emails, Flights, Deals, and Deadlines

The corporate treadmill never stops—and neither do the temptations: airport lounges, hotel buffets, business lunches, room service, cocktails. Add to that the emotional undercurrents from personal life, and the pressure only builds.

Take Rhea, for instance, a young executive travelling for back-to-back meetings. It's 11 p.m., she's exhausted, deadlines loom and loneliness from the road sets in. She grabs room service, barely noticing what's on her plate and eats quickly just to satisfy hunger and move on. Meals like these become rushed, forgettable and disconnected from real satisfaction. That feeling of truly enjoying a meal? It's lost.

But what if just seven conscious breaths before eating could help you take back control—without giving up the foods you love? Yes, even that flaky Danish pastry from the executive lounge.

That's the power of 7 Breaths to Slimming—a technique designed to meet you exactly where you are, grounding you, slowing your pace and helping you to savour the moment.

Why It Matters

Ironically, it's in high-pressure environments that eating with awareness matters most. Stress blurs your body's natural signals. It floods your system with cortisol—the stress hormone—which increases cravings for calorie-dense foods and promotes fat storage, especially around the midsection. Even with the best intentions, corporate life throws curveballs:

- A fresh juice morning turns into a cocktail-heavy night.
- Flights get delayed, meetings drag on, dinners stack up.
- And your weight goals? Left trailing behind.

But maybe the solution isn't restriction—it's attention. By actively engaging your breath, you signal to your nervous system that you're safe, down-regulating the stress response and calming the hormonal rollercoaster that fuels stress-eating. Slimming isn't about perfection. It's about presence. And when the world keeps rushing, your breath gives you the chance to pause. (Your brain, however, might still be replaying that awkward moment from last week's presentation.)

The 7 Breaths Practice and The Mini Breath

Whether you're mid-flight, mid-meeting or mid-mayhem, this simple breathing habit helps reset your mind and body—anytime, anywhere.

The 7 Breaths Practice: Before every meal, take seven slow, intentional breaths. Each breath gives you a chance to pause, refocus and realign with your slimming goals. It's a moment of calm before you nourish your body—a gentle refresh for your internal operating system.

So how do you regain control in a world of rushed meals and constant temptation? That's where the 7 Breaths Practice comes in.

The Mini Breath

Pressed for time? Just take the final three breaths of the full practice. A quick reset. A powerful anchor. You don't need to change your surroundings—only how you show up in them. It's subtle enough that no one in the office will notice.

Real people. Real shifts.

I've lived the corporate hustle. I know what it's like to grab quick bites between high-stakes projects and red-eye flights. My diet used to be mostly lattes and snacks from airport lounges and kiosks. Determined to regain control without falling into the trap of rigid diets, I created 7 Breaths to Slimming—a simple, breath-based technique practised before meals. It worked for me. And when I introduced it in corporate wellness workshops, the results were powerful.

Sonal, 42, HR Head: 'I used to snack through meetings. Now I pause to breathe. Half the time, I'm not hungry—just stressed.

And now I have a legitimate excuse not to share the office treats.'

Vikram, 39, Investment Banker: 'Client dinners ruined my mornings. The breath practice grounds me. I feel more in control and less likely to wake up regretting that extra dessert.'

Elena, 29, Startup Co-Founder: 'Airport pastries were my comfort food. Now I breathe before ordering. Sometimes I skip them. Sometimes I don't. But now I choose—with clarity.'

Ramesh, 48, CEO: 'I'm a foodie. Diets don't work for me. But this? This breath practice I can do—and I don't have to give up my beloved biryani. I just enjoy it more consciously.'

These aren't dramatic overhauls. They're small, conscious shifts. Tiny pauses. Lasting change. That's the promise of this breath practice.

Common Corporate Hurdles—and How to Elegantly Jump Them

- 'No time for breathing. I'm too busy conquering the world!' (Says everyone with a bursting inbox.) Here's the good news: the 7 Breaths—or even the 3 Mini Breaths—take less time than scrolling through your phone. Blink, breathe, done.
- 'My colleagues will think I've lost it.' Good news again! This is a covert operation. Breathing is subtle and internal. It's a reset button, not a performance—unless you want to start a wellness trend at work.
- 'It feels silly.' Maybe. But what's sillier—feeling sluggish, stressed and stuck in a diet spiral or taking a few calming breaths that actually work? You decide.

Post-Meal Lethargy

That afternoon slump—the yawns, the brain fog, the endless craving for coffee—is real. I've felt it too. It's often paired with the strong belief that every office should come with a nap room—and a do-not-disturb sign. Instead of reaching for sugar or caffeine, try this: take the 7 Breaths before your meal. It supports digestion and helps you stay sharp long after lunch.

Priya, VP Finance: 'Before the breath practice, I couldn't survive the afternoon without sugar or coffee. Now I feel alert without them.'

Ramesh, National Sales Manager: 'I'm more present in meetings. The breath practice helped me beat the slump and stay on track with my weight goals.'

It's like flipping a switch—from fog to focus. A powerful, portable reset.

The Hidden Cost of Corporate Eating

Success isn't owned. It's leased. And rent is due every day.

—J.J. Watt

And sometimes that rent shows up as an expanding waistline. In high-performance environments, eating becomes reactive:

- Skipped breakfasts ('I'll grab something at the office' usually means a stale croissant)
- Grab-and-go lunches (eaten while replying to emails, naturally)
- Reward dinners that spiral (you deserve it after that brutal project)

- Cookie crunching during calls (they're distracting, so you barely notice you've inhaled the whole packet)
- 'Just one more' cocktail (because…networking, obviously)
- Airport munching without a second thought (duty-free chocolate—because calories don't count in transit, right?)

Then comes the guilt—the frantic search for the nearest juice cleanse. Then the crash diets—which last about as long as a New Year's resolution. Then the burnout—which, predictably, lands you right back in the cookie jar. So how do you break the cycle?

Five Everyday Eating Traps—and Simple Swaps

- **Meeting Munch Trap**
  Trigger: Snacking during brainstorms
  Swap: Do the Mini Breath practice before reaching for the office cookie. Feel the space it creates and ask yourself: 'Is this hunger—or just habit and legendary office snacks?'
- **Desk-Dining Dilemma**
  Trigger: Eating while working
  Swap: Block time for a proper meal. Start with the 7 Breaths Practice. Let each breath remind your brain: 'This is my food moment, not my work moment. Eyes on the prize—your delicious meal, not the spreadsheet.'
- **Elevator Snack Spiral**
  Trigger: Tea break turns into chips
  Swap: Decide your snack before heading to the pantry. Do the breath practice at the door. Use those breaths to ask: 'Do I actually want this or am I just bored in business casual?'
- **Travel Trap**

Trigger: 'I deserve this—I'm travelling'
Swap: Pack smart snacks. Do the Mini Breath when cravings hit. Use those breaths to decide if that airport puff is a true need—or just a travel-induced comfort habit. (Truth be told, airline food rarely inspires real cravings.)

- **Celebration Loop**
  Trigger: Wins, birthdays, festivals
  Swap: Enjoy the cake—but begin with the breath practice. Awareness first. Even in celebration, a few breaths help you truly savour the moment—so the joy comes from connection, not just the sugar rush. And you're far less likely to wake up in a frosting fog.

Why This Works

This isn't about restriction—we're not taking away your cake. It's about intention. You don't need to skip buffets or refuse dessert. You just need a brief pause to breathe and reclaim your choice. It's like unlocking a superpower—for your stomach. The pause helps you reset, reconnect and stay aligned with your goals. Your breath is always with you—no matter the chaos, the deadlines or the five-hour video calls with no clear agenda. With every conscious inhale, you reclaim your presence. And with presence comes power—the power to eat with intention, live with purpose and lead with calm.

A simple breath-based reset can shift everything.

Team Wellness in Action: The Power of Breath

During a tech firm's wellness week, I introduced the 7 Breaths Practice. No diets. No rules. Just a simple pause. Within two weeks, everything changed:

- Sugar cravings dropped, and the office candy dish started looking lonely.
- Water replaced chips—a surprising but welcome shift.
- Teams turned it into a game with a 'breathe & bite' tracker—because everything's better with a leaderboard and a little healthy competition.
- Client dinners became easier—less overeating, more enjoyment.
- Eating slowed down, focus sharpened and reactions softened—even during heated debates over font choices.

This wasn't just about weight. It was about finding calm in the chaos. When practised together, wellness becomes part of the culture. And who knows—maybe even fewer passive-aggressive emails. Seven breaths. A pause. One small shift at a time. That's how lasting habits evolve.

Make It a Team Shift

Imagine if your team's next KPI wasn't just productivity—but presence. Small culture shifts can spark big change:

- Encourage friendly check-ins: 'Did you do your breath reset today?'
- Share buddy nudges—sometimes we all need a gentle reminder, especially before diving into the snack drawer.

Small shifts ripple. A few consistent pauses can create a shared rhythm. Before long, it becomes part of your team's DNA.

What to Know

The office isn't the problem. Mindless behaviour is. Your brain on default mode is far more dangerous than any spreadsheet error. You don't need a new diet. You need new decisions—and every decision starts with awareness. Even the Mini Breath practice can break the stress-eating cycle and signal to your body: 'I'm safe. I'm present. I choose.' And sometimes, 'I choose not to eat that questionable leftover pizza.' Whether you're leading a team or boarding a flight—the breath-based reset is your power.

Your Personal Corporate Wellness Mission

Even if your company hasn't caught on to the power of breath (yet!), you can start your own quiet revolution. Make the 7 Breaths Practice your personal secret weapon. Before your next meeting, before reaching for that snack, before replying to that stressful email, just pause. Your body, your mind and your waistline will thank you.

NamitaSpeaks

Commit to the breath practice. It's not just about what you lose on the scale. The stillness you cultivate with every breath also sharpens your focus, enhances your decision-making and boosts your emotional resilience. In a demanding corporate world, this isn't just a slimming trick; it's a strategic advantage. You show up clearer, calmer, and more in control, not just of your plate but your entire day. Because thriving at work isn't just about doing more; it's about showing up as your best self, every single day.

4

Dining out

'Can I still dine out and lose weight?' It's a question I hear time and again—usually accompanied by a hopeful, slightly desperate look.

When I first shared 7 Breaths to Slimming with a friend, her eyes lit up with relief. 'Finally,' she said, 'something that doesn't involve green smoothies, detox juices or giving up everything I love!'

Let's be real: a life without your favourite food is no life at all. But then came the question many quietly ask:

'What about eating out?'

She loves exploring new restaurants, savouring menus, soaking in the experience. For many of us, dining out is more than just food—it's joy, discovery, connection. It's celebrating with friends, sealing business deals or simply enjoying precious moments with loved ones.

And in those moments, the pressure to eat, drink and be merry—often excessively—can feel immense.

Her worry was real and familiar: 'If I want to lose weight, do I have to give all that up?'

That fear is understandable. Somewhere along the way, we've been taught that health and happiness can't share a plate. That slimming down means sacrifice, guilt, and 'cheat days'—if eating out is allowed at all.

But here's what I know—from my journey and from guiding

many others: You don't have to choose between your lifestyle and your goals. You don't need to give up your favourite dishes, your social life or spontaneous dinners.

You just need one simple shift: awareness. Not rules. Not restriction. Not punishment. Just presence—anchored by breath.

When you take those conscious breaths, you create a micro-space—a moment for your true power of choice to emerge, unclouded by impulse or external pressure. And when you pause to breathe before you eat, something shifts. You slow down. You allow your senses to truly engage with the taste of your food.

This conscious savouring often leads to greater satisfaction—with smaller portions. You reset. You reconnect. You choose with clarity. And that's where real transformation begins.

Dining out is about joy, connection and celebration, but it can also be tricky. Oversized portions, multiple courses, alcohol, sharing plates and the social pressure to keep up with everyone's pace can make it easy to overeat or lose awareness.

This is where a simple pause, taking a few mindful breaths before the first bite, can help. It grounds you, slows your pace, and lets you stay present, so you enjoy the experience without feeling pressured or guilty.

Breaking Free from Yo-Yo Dieting

Yo-yo dieting, also known as weight cycling, is when you lose weight on a restrictive diet, gain it back once the diet ends and then start dieting all over again. It's a repeated loop of losing and regaining weight, just like a yo-yo going up and down. It can feel tiring, discouraging and like you're always starting over.

The idea of a 'cheat meal' comes from diets that are rigid, restrictive and joyless. It's like being stuck in a strict boarding school…but for your stomach.

But when you eat with balance and intention, there's nothing to cheat on. The guilt fades. The craving cycle softens. Peace replaces punishment.

So, here's a question I often ask: Would you rather stay stuck in the yo-yo cycle—strict on weekdays, splurging on weekends, dreading the scale every Monday, only to start over again?

It's exhausting, isn't it?

Or would you prefer a rhythm that's sustainable, gentle and joyful? A rhythm where it doesn't matter if it's Monday or Saturday, homemade or your favourite restaurant—because your choices consistently support your slimming journey with ease and grace?

7 Breaths to Slimming invites you into that rhythm. To pause. To breathe. To choose with presence. And most importantly—to enjoy the journey.

Why Willpower Isn't Enough

Willpower is like a battery—it drains fast. Especially after a long day of pretending to listen in exhaustive meetings.

Science backs it: the more decisions you make, the quicker your willpower fades.

So, what's the real game-changer? Structure. The unsung hero of all successful endeavours—including fitting into skinny jeans.

Your brain craves predictability. It thrives on habits and systems that reduce decision fatigue and free up mental energy.

That's why true success—at work, in relationships or

on your slimming journey—doesn't come from bursts of motivation. It comes from building small, repeatable habits that carry you forward, even on tough days.

Picture this: You don't have to feel like it to make the right choice. You don't wait for motivation to strike. You simply follow the system or structure you've created.

The habit kicks in. The action happens. And you move forward—calmly, consistently.

From that freedom, real transformation begins. Structure fuels progress. Discipline just starts the engine.

How Slim People Stay in Sync

Have you noticed how naturally slim people, even in indulgent settings, eat with quiet confidence?

They enjoy their food—but stay careful. They eat with control and usually stop before they feel full. Their choices subtly align with their slimming goals.

Over time, this attuned listening builds deep trust in their body's signals, making portion control feel natural, not forced.

And when they do overdo it, they adjust—maybe skipping the next meal or choosing something lighter.

Why? Because their body speaks to them. It signals fullness, discomfort, bloating. And they listen.

That's exactly what the breath practice teaches you: to pause. To savour each bite more fully, ensuring maximum pleasure from less food. To sense. To stop before discomfort turns into regret.

To avoid that heavy, bloated feeling after overeating. And if you slip? If you lose track? It's okay. It happens to the best of us—especially when faced with a particularly tempting dessert menu.

This journey isn't a test. It's a process. A lapse isn't failure—it's a cue to reset.

What throws most people off isn't the indulgence—it's the guilt that follows. And that guilt becomes the real derailment.

The key is simple: come back to the breath; come back to yourself.

It's Not about Perfection—It's about Awareness

Eating patterns are learned behaviours. Your body listens to your direction.

The real question is: Are you paying attention? Or are you just mindlessly consuming that second helping?

Weekend triggers? Meet conscious choices.

'I can't wait to try that new pizzeria… Or maybe Lebanese? Thai? Tandoori?'

Sound familiar?

Weekends often arrive dressed as temptations—brunches, social dinners, family feasts. It can feel like a whirlwind when you're trying to stay on track. Like navigating a bustling marketplace…blindfolded.

But here's the truth: you don't have to say no to life. You just need to show up with presence.

Here Are 5 Common Weekend Traps—and How to Breathe through Them

1. **The Social Spiral**
   Trigger: Friends ordering round after round of food and drink
   Response: Before the first bite or sip, take your 7 Breaths silently. Let them anchor you. This quiet moment helps

you observe social cues without feeling pressured to mimic them. You stay engaged in the conversation—but grounded in your own choices.

2. **The Family Feast Trap**
   Trigger: Overeating out of love, tradition, or habit ('But grandma made it—you must have more!')
   Response: Begin with your breath. Feel the love behind the meal. Then serve yourself just enough. Honour the affection—but honour your body too.
3. **The 'I Deserve This' Drift**
   Trigger: 'I've earned this!'—especially after a stressful week
   Response: Yes, you have. But joy doesn't have to come with regret. Breathe. Then ask: 'What would truly feel good right now?' More often than not, the answer is peace—not excess.
4. **The Buffet Blackout**
   Trigger: The overwhelm of an all-you-can-eat spread; eyes bigger than your stomach
   Response: Step back. Breathe. Let the excitement settle. Then choose with intention. You don't need everything—you just need what truly satisfies.
5. **The 'I'll-Start-Monday' Mindset**
   Trigger: 'Let me binge now—I'll be good later'
   Response: Tempting, but self-sabotaging. Pause. Breathe. Then ask: 'What can I choose now that my future self will thank me for?' That's real progress.

Whether you use the full 7 Breaths Practice or a shorter version—the Mini Breath—the power lies in the pause. Because nothing changes...if nothing changes.

Covert Breathing Operations: Restaurant Edition

Eating out is a joy—but practising breathing openly at the table can sometimes feel awkward or draw attention. That's where 'covert breathing operations' come in: simple, discreet breathing techniques you can weave into your dining routine without anyone noticing.

'Covert' means secret or hidden—these are your low-key, behind-the-scenes breath pauses that keep you grounded and in control while blending naturally into the rhythm of your meal.

Think of them as your secret weapon for making conscious choices with ease, even in social or busy settings.

Here's how to use these covert breathing moments:

- While looking at the menu: Take your breaths as you browse, clearing your mind and calming cravings so you can order with clarity.
- Waiting for your order: Instead of scrolling on your phone or feeling impatient, use this pause to centre yourself with your breath practice.
- Between courses: A perfect time for a Mini Breath pause to check in with your fullness signals before deciding if you want more.

These subtle breath pauses help you stay connected to your body's needs, reduce impulse eating and support mindful, joyful dining—wherever you are.

Restaurant Survival Kit: Traps and Swaps

Whether it's the warm bread basket, a never-ending menu or the pressure to finish everything on your plate, restaurants are full of subtle cues that can nudge you out of your centred state.

This kit is your quick-reference guide to common triggers and easy breath-based responses—so you stay calm, connected and in control, no matter what's on the menu.

- The Bread Basket Black Hole
  Trigger: That complimentary bread basket arriving too early and being too tempting (it's like they know your weakness)
  Response: Take a Mini Breath pause as soon as it lands on the table. Consciously observe the presence of the bread instead of automatically reaching for it.
- The 'Everything-on-the-Menu' Syndrome
  Trigger: Overwhelmed by too many delicious choices, leading to ordering too much (because FOMO applies to food too)
  Response: Before opening the menu, take a few calming breaths. As you read, take a Mini Breath pause for each dish that tempts you, sensing if it aligns with your true hunger and goals.
- The 'Clean-Plate-Club' Pressure
  Trigger: Feeling obligated to finish everything, even if you're full—as wasting food feels like a crime
  Response: Mid-meal, take a deep breath check-in. Listen to your body's fullness cues. It's okay to leave food behind. Your breath practice empowers you to honour your body's signals over external pressures or old habits.

Why This Works

This isn't about restriction—we're still friends with dessert. It's about intention. You don't need to skip the buffet or deny the cake. You just need the pause—a moment to breathe and reconnect with your inner compass.

Your breath is more than a calming tool—it's a quiet act of self-leadership. It brings you back when the noise around you gets loud.

Even when the menu's overwhelming or the table is full of temptations, your breath anchors you. With each breath, you step back into alignment.

NamitaSpeaks

Eating out isn't the enemy. (Phew!) Losing control isn't the end. When you return to your breath, you reclaim your power—quietly, gently and without judgement. So next time you're at a brunch, buffet or celebration, ask yourself: What would the wisest, kindest version of me choose right now? Then breathe. Let the answer rise. Let the breath practice guide you. Because you're not just slimming your body—you're strengthening your spirit.

5

The Healthy Eating Trap: Eating Right—but Getting It Wrong

The hidden traps in 'healthy' food: ever eaten all the 'right' foods and still gained weight?

You followed the rules, read the labels, stocked up on gluten-free, sugar-free, organic everything. Maybe even found a kale smoothie recipe that didn't make you cry. But the results? Confusing at best. Frustrating at worst.

Welcome to the healthy eating trap—where labels look angelic, but calories lurk like hidden landmines in a five-star hotel.

Why This Isn't Another Diet

The problem isn't a lack of information, it's too much. Keto, Paleo, Vegan, Intermittent Fasting... Every diet has its cheerleaders and critics, promising transformation if followed perfectly. But what counts as 'healthy' varies wildly depending on the diet, the body, the mindset.

What one diet calls a superfood—nuts, seeds, jaggery, multigrain, cheese, might be off-limits in another. Even universally agreed upon wholesome foods don't fit all diets or bodies. So, when people say, 'just eat healthy', it can feel confusing, even overwhelming. Because healthy isn't one-size-fits-all. It depends on your diet. Your body. Your mindset.

Here's where most people struggle: sticking to a plan with discipline. When that falters, they jump to the next trend, hoping it'll be the one. What overwhelmed me wasn't the diets themselves, it was the noise around them. The rigid rules. The guilt. The fear of 'breaking' the plan. The illusion that there's one perfect way to eat. This pursuit of perfection often leads to anxiety around food, turning a nourishing act into a constant test.

Through the breath practice in this book, you can gently release rigidity and reconnect with yourself. That's when I had an insight: What people need isn't another plan. They need to reconnect with their own inner guide.

7 Breaths to Slimming isn't about telling you what to eat. It's about helping you listen, to your hunger, your satisfaction, your body. And it starts with one of the simplest tools you already have: your breath.

A Cautionary Tale: The 'Healthy' Diet That Backfired

Let me share a true story. Someone I know, full of enthusiasm, decided to lose weight. She called one morning, excited: 'Your chef makes the best salads, it doesn't even feel like diet food!'

She then stocked her kitchen with everything 'healthy': low-calorie snacks, sugar-free desserts, gluten-free crackers, almond, soya and skimmed milk, avocados, green vegetables, olive oil, granola, jaggery, nuts, tofu... All the right buzzwords. She followed the plan with dedication. But a month later, when she stepped on the scale, she had gained two kilos.

Frustrated, she asked, 'But how could I gain weight on a healthy diet?' The answer—it wasn't just what she ate, but how much. Healthy foods are still calorie-laden. We often fall prey to the 'healthy halo' effect—believing that because something is wholesome (like that delicious organic granola), we can eat unlimited quantities without consequence.

Spoiler alert: calories still count, even when they come from good intentions. Think about it: a small handful of almonds is healthy. But an entire bag? That's more calories than a full meal. A drizzle of olive oil is good. A generous pour? That's hundreds of hidden calories. Nuts, granola, jaggery are all good in moderation. But too much of anything adds up.

This is where portion control comes in, not as restriction, but as respect. For your body. For your hunger. For your goals. Portion control can feel tricky because modern meals are often oversized; emotions influence when and how much we eat, and distractions make it easy to lose track of fullness. However, all it takes to begin is a pause and a breath.

That conscious pause enabled by your breath practice helps you slow down and register what a respectful portion feels like in your hand and on your plate before it even reaches your mouth.

'Do You Hear It?' Step into any conversation about health, and you'll hear:

Keto works for me, swear by it! High-protein is the secret.

I eat before 7 p.m., that's my trick. Ayurveda changed everything.

Go vegan! The weight just drops. Gluten-free, lactose-free, that's the slimming solution!

Everyone's found their 'magic formula'. Everyone's convinced they're right even if it's just a phase that happened to work. So naturally, you wonder: What's the right way for me? The truth? There is no universal 'right'. There is only your right. Your rhythm. Your body. Your choices.

To begin listening, try this: at your next meal, after your seven breaths, consciously scan your body. Where do you feel hunger? How does your first bite feel? Pay attention to these subtle cues—this is your inner guide speaking.

How the 7 Breaths Practice Helps

Before every meal or snack, try this:

Pause.
Breathe—take seven slow, grounding breaths.
Ask yourself: Am I truly hungry…or just reacting?
Is your stomach growling like a hungry lion or are you bored, stressed or just eyeing that tempting snack on your colleague's desk?
Decide from there.
Or try the Mini Breath practice—a short, intentional reset to bring yourself back to centre.

Clarity begins with breath. Control follows.

NamitaSpeaks

Let awareness guide your portions. Weight loss isn't about binge-eating 'healthy' foods. It's about focus. And it's about experiencing true satisfaction—not just being 'full'. Your breath practice helps you slow down. It allows you to truly register the nourishment in each bite. This helps you feel satisfied—with less. You hold the tools to make every bite count.

SECTION FOUR

Foundations of Lasting Change—Sustaining Your Transformation

In the previous sections, you learned the fundamental steps of the 7 Breaths technique and understood its immediate benefits. As we move into Section 4, the focus shifts from *how to do it* to *how to sustain it*. Here, you'll discover how the calm, clarity and control you've begun to cultivate are integrated into your daily life.

Your breath practice now evolves from a simple technique into a true foundation for lasting change, supporting your slimming journey with calm, inner strength and enduring confidence.

1

Long-Term Benefits: Breath as Your Anchor

When was the last time you truly paused before eating—just a moment to breathe deeply, settle your mind and listen to your body? Most of us rush through meals distracted, stressed or disconnected. Yet, it's in this simple pause—this conscious breath—that transformation begins. Unlike fleeting diet fads that promise quick wins but lead to yo-yo setbacks, 7 Breaths to Slimming offers a sustainable anchor.

It helps you build habits that last a lifetime. This isn't about quick fixes or drastic diets (because let's be honest—who wants to survive another week on cabbage soup?). It's about rediscovering a gentle rhythm—one that brings your mind, body and emotions into sync and invites lasting change from within.

It's about caring for yourself with kindness not punishing restriction. It's about creating habits that support a vibrant, balanced life—one relaxed breath at a time. With each intentional breath, you lay the foundation for a healthier relationship with food, grounded in awareness, not anxiety, in connection, not control.

The Science and Soul of Slimming

Eating in a relaxed state of mind and practising portion control can significantly enhance digestion and support heart health. In 7 Breaths to Slimming, *Namita Jain highlights the power of simple, sustained well-being.*

—Dr Ashwin Mehta, Padma Bhushan awardee and leading cardiologist

The breath practice becomes your compass, helping you stay grounded and intentional with every bite. Breath by breath, you move closer to your destination—not through deprivation, but through conscious, empowered action.

And of course, if your goal is to lose weight, it's a valid and practical one—you deserve to see results. So why not choose a path that leads you there—with clarity, balance and confidence?

That inspiration led me to create a series of health videos, with a message that reaches beyond the surface: slimming isn't just physical.

When I was talking to individuals and listening to their struggles, I realized that real transformation isn't about deprivation or willpower—it's about connection. Most people weren't failing diets, they were simply disconnected from their breath, their bodies and their inner wisdom.

If it were just about food or exercise, most of us would've reached our ideal form by now. But real transformation begins from within. It's not about vanity or unrealistic ideals. It's about feeling aligned—physically, mentally, emotionally, and psychologically. It's about reclaiming a sense of control and confidence, one breath at a time.

In that spirit, *7 Breaths to Slimming* was never intended to be just another diet book. Instead, it's an invitation to experience a new rhythm—a breath-based method that aligns your mind and body before each meal.

This simple practice, paired with affirmations, empowers

you to take control of your choices. It gently guides you toward balance, awareness and a sustainable slimming path.

At its core, this practice is built on three timeless principles: relaxation, discipline and portion control. These are not new concepts. They are rooted in tradition and supported by science. After all, success in any area of life requires discipline. But discipline doesn't need to be harsh or restrictive.

The real power lies in learning to listen to your body—staying aligned with what truly works for you. Over time, living with intention and ease becomes second nature.

A Holistic Approach

This breath-based method supports your entire well-being by calming your nervous system and reducing stress, which naturally enhances your daily habits. It fosters a state of balance that encourages healthier movement, deeper rest and more intentional self-care. Here's how:

1. **Physical Benefits**
    - Activates the parasympathetic nervous system—your body's natural 'rest--and-digest' mode. Finally, a way to tell your inner stress monster to take a break.
    - Prepares the digestive tract to process food more efficiently.
    - Encourages eating in response to real hunger, not stress triggers like a tight deadline or a tense meeting.
2. **Mental Clarity**
    - Clears the mental fog—because a clear head is better than a caffeine overload.
    - Helps you pause before impulsive decisions (like hitting 'order' on that midnight pizza).

- Replaces stress with intention, so you choose nourishment instead of numbness.

3. **Emotional Resilience**
   - Brings calm during moments of emotional overwhelm—so a bad day doesn't have to mean a bad diet.
   - Builds inner strength, patience and self-compassion.
   - Makes you less reactive and more composed when it comes to both food and feelings.

Healing Begins with a Breath

The power of the breath practice isn't just something you feel—it's something your body registers on a cellular level. Each breath sends a signal of safety and calm, helping restore internal balance and bring harmony to your entire system.

Let's take a closer look at how this practice impacts your body and mind:

The Heart

- Calms the heart rate
- Lowers blood pressure
- Strengthens emotional resilience—reducing stress that burdens your heart

The Lungs

- Expands lung capacity
- Improves oxygen flow
- Helps release physical and emotional toxins through breath

The Mind

- Sharpens focus
- Encourages positive self-talk through affirmations
- Replaces anxiety with clarity

The Emotions

- Creates space between feeling and action
- Encourages conscious, compassionate eating
- Builds emotional intelligence and inner peace

With each breath, you're not just nourishing your body—you're healing from the inside out.

How Breath Supports Sustainable Slimming

Science backs what ancient wisdom has always known: the way you breathe shapes how your body stores, burns and responds to food. Here's how breath creates a long-lasting slimming effect:

- Activates Fat-Burning Pathways: Regular breathwork helps your body burn fat more efficiently—even at rest. Deep breathing improves oxygen delivery to cells, supporting metabolic activity and fat oxidation.
- Reduces Belly Fat by Lowering Cortisol: Chronic stress spikes cortisol, which encourages abdominal fat storage. Conscious breathing activates the parasympathetic nervous system, calming stress hormones and reducing fat accumulation over time.
- Improves Insulin Sensitivity: Stress management through breath helps regulate blood sugar levels and insulin response, key factors in reducing fat storage and cravings.
- Boosts Mitochondrial Health: Mitochondria are your body's energy engines. Breathwork, especially slow diaphragmatic breathing, enhances oxygen supply to cells, improving energy output and metabolic rate.
- Builds Consistency and Resilience: The more you

breathe with awareness, the more consistent you become with your eating habits. This practice gently replaces impulsive, unconscious patterns with sustainable choices, acting as a shield against future cravings and emotional eating. Each intentional breath rewires your brain to pause, reflect and choose, laying down new neural pathways that support lasting change.

- Supports Hormonal Balance: Breath influences hormones beyond cortisol, including ghrelin and leptin, which regulate hunger and satiety, helping you feel full at the right time and avoid overeating.

Beyond the Scale: The Ripple Effect

Slimming isn't about extremes, it's about alignment. And breath is the bridge between your inner calm and outer transformation. Breath practice impacts:

- Your relationship with food, which shifts from guilt to grace
- Your stress response, which transforms from chaos to calm
- Your awareness, which deepens, extending far beyond mealtimes
- Your choices, which become conscious, not compulsive

This is empowerment. This is intentional living.

A Paradigm Shift

We've been taught that health is a battlefield full of restriction and rigidity (a battle most of us are constantly losing, it seems). But what if health didn't have to be hard? The 7 Breaths Practice offers a new method. No force. No shame. Just space—space to pause, space to breathe, space to choose. Instead of pushing your body into submission, you invite it to collaborate with you. You listen. You lead. You align.

Who This Practice Is for

Whether you're just starting out or well along your way in the slimming journey, this breath-based method fits seamlessly into your life—no equipment, no pressure. It's about showing up, tuning into your body and leading your path with kindness and confidence. One breath at a time.

Real Life: Voices from the Journey

These scientific principles, when consistently applied through the simple act of breathing, translate into profound, real-world changes. The proof is in the renewed vitality and the success stories of those who have embraced this practice.

Over time, I've had the honour of assisting a diverse group of people on their slimming journeys through seminars, workshops, retreats and one-on-one sessions. When I created 7 Breaths to Slimming to support my weight loss and began sharing it with others, the feedback was immediate and heartfelt.

> *'I always believed slimming meant starving. But just pausing to breathe helped me tune in to what I needed—not just food, but calm. I started this during a hospital wellness workshop with Namita, and it's now part of my daily life.'*
>
> —Dr Sneha Deshmukh, 42, paediatrician

'Stress-eating was my weakness. Practising 7 Breaths before meals gave me a sense of control I hadn't felt in years. I first heard of the practice during a corporate wellness session, and I've been consistent ever since.'

—Avinash Mehra, 38, investment banker

'As a new mom, I struggled with emotional eating and post-baby weight. This practice grounded me—it gave me space to breathe, pause, and respond with self-compassion. It all began with a consultation with Namita.'

—Anita Kulkarni, 33, marketing consultant

NamitaSpeaks

The breath practice goes beyond slimming—it calls you into a life of presence, clarity and calm. Every breath is a reminder of your strength. Every affirmation a step towards your best self. This is not a destination—it's a lifelong evolution. Keep breathing. Keep shining.

2

The Gut-Brain Connection: Where Calm Breath Meets Conscious Eating

Did you know your gut and brain are constantly in conversation? It's like an ongoing text exchange—sometimes your brain is in panic mode, sending urgent messages, and your gut calmly replies, 'Message received.' This continuous dialogue plays a major role in how you digest food, regulate emotions and even manage cravings. So, who's the secret messenger?

The vagus nerve is a powerful superhighway linking your gut and brain in a two-way conversation. In today's fast-paced, high-stress world, learning to activate this nerve consciously is a true game-changer. It's increasingly recognized for its profound impact on overall well-being—physical, emotional and mental.

When this connection is calm and clear, digestion flows smoothly, moods stay balanced, and eating feels natural and satisfying. You feel a lightness after meals, sustained energy and a mental clarity that wasn't there when you were eating on autopilot. But stress and rushed meals can scramble this message, leading to bloating, cravings and emotional eating.

Here's the good news: your breath is the key to tuning into this vital gut-brain conversation. By activating the vagus nerve through slow, relaxed breathing, you calm both your mind and your digestive system at once. This simple act primes your body to digest better, reduce emotional eating and stabilize cravings.

Breathe, Then Begin

> *'A calm mind is a calm abdomen, and a calm abdomen is key for good absorption and digestion. In this book, Namita encourages a breath practice to activate the body's rest-and-digest response.'*
>
> **—Dr Prasanna Shah, leading gastroenterologist**

Here, you're invited to shift from feeling full to feeling light, with a practice so simple, it begins with your breath. Because true nourishment doesn't start with what's on your plate; it starts with how present you are. When you pause before a meal, you create space for awareness. And in that space, portion control becomes effortless, digestion improves and your relationship with food transforms.

You'll find that conscious eating, even with smaller portions, amplifies the joy and satisfaction from every single bite, making food taste even better! Before you reach for your fork, reach inward. Breathe. Then begin.

Subodh Tiwari, CEO of Kaivalyadhama, one of India's oldest and most respected yoga institutes, expresses it beautifully: *'Pausing for a brief prayer before meals brings a sense of calm. It is a gesture of gratitude for the nourishment we receive and an act of inner harmony.'*

This simple pause, quiet and intentional, transforms eating into a sacred ritual. It invites presence over distraction, awareness over impulse. In that calm space, true nourishment begins—not from hunger or habit, but from balance.

For those who already pause to offer a prayer before meals, the 7 Breaths Practice can flow seamlessly before it. Together, they deepen the moment, bringing calm, clarity and conscious connection to your meal.

In Practice: 7 Breaths to Slimming

The practice of taking seven slow breaths—or even doing the Mini Breath practice, which is a shorter version—before a meal:

1. Soothes the nervous system by activating the vagus nerve through deep breathing, which in turn improves gut motility and digestion.
2. Helps you set clear intentions, enhancing awareness around eating habits.
3. Supports portion control, making weight management more sustainable. This isn't about restriction, it's about realignment. Breath becomes a bridge: from stress to calm, from compulsion to choice.

Less Is More: Listening to the Body's SOS

Many clients share the same refrain:

- 'I feel so sleepy after lunch that I can't focus.'
- 'Every time I overeat, I feel bloated and acidic.'
- 'I just want to lie down after a heavy meal—it drains my energy.'

You're not alone. These aren't minor discomforts—they're the body's SOS signals. When we overeat, blood rushes to the gut and away from the brain, leading to brain fog, fatigue and mood dips.

Clients frequently ask:

Q: Is 7 Breaths to Slimming a breath technique to lose weight?

A: Yes—it's a simple, breath-based method that helps build discipline.

Q: Discipline for what?

A: For portion awareness, mindful eating and staying consistent with healthy habits. This isn't about white-knuckling through restrictions. It's about cultivating an inner discipline that feels natural—gentle self-regulation born from awareness, not force. You begin to eat less and make more conscious choices, effortlessly.

Q: And how does that help?

A: That's your secret weapon. When portion control and awareness become second nature, slimming becomes sustainable.

Q: Should the breath practice continue even after reaching weight goals?

A: Yes. The 7 Breaths Practice isn't just for weight loss; it's a lifestyle anchor. Continuing it, along with portion control and movement, helps you stay light, balanced and in tune with your body long after the numbers on the scale have settled.

The Hunger Myth

It convinces us to eat when we're not truly hungry, to crave without cause and to override our internal compass. It clouds judgement, leads to overeating and leaves us disconnected from our bodies. It's important to remember that sometimes true hunger can still arise even after a recent meal, especially with intense physical activity or growth. The key is to truly tune in, rather than dismiss, your body's signals. But here's the good news: awareness, anchored by breath, can break the spell.

The Three Types of False Hunger

1. Emotional Hunger: triggered by stress, anxiety, loneliness, boredom, or even celebration. Food becomes comfort, not nourishment. 'I've had a tough day—I deserve this.' Or, 'I feel empty—let me fill the gap.'
2. Habitual Hunger: programmed by routine rather than need. 'It's 9 p.m.—time for dessert.' Or, 'I always snack while watching TV.'
3. Environmental Hunger: stimulated by smells, sights or social settings. 'The popcorn smells amazing—I need some.' 'Everyone's eating—I might as well join.'

None of these is wrong. But when they control our eating patterns, we lose connection with real hunger. The breath practice is your built-in lie detector. It helps you listen, not just to your appetite, but to your actual needs.

Redefining Fullness

From childhood, we're conditioned to 'finish the plate' or 'not waste food'. These well-meaning cues often lead us to override the body's gentle signal of 'enough', waiting instead for the loud discomfort of 'too much'. The 7 Breaths Practice helps you reconnect with your satiety cues. It teaches you to recognize:

- A subtle, satisfying sense of 'just enough'
- A light, comfortable feeling in the belly
- A natural impulse to pause

The Magic of Eighty Per Cent

What does 'eighty per cent full' feel like? It's intuitive. With consistent breath and awareness, your body begins to guide you. When you stop at eighty per cent, you may notice:

- Smoother digestion
- Stable energy levels
- Balanced blood sugar

A study in the *Journal of Nutrition* found that eating to satiety—rather than to fullness—supports lower calorie intake, improved metabolic markers and even healthy ageing.[7]

Scientific Insight

Portion control isn't about restriction—it's about physiology. Here's how your body responds:

- Improved insulin sensitivity helps avoid energy crashes
- Better gut motility reduces bloating and reflux
- Balanced hunger hormones (like leptin) help prevent overeating
- Reduced post-meal fatigue leaves you feeling vibrant

Even reducing portions by just ten to twenty per cent can lead to sustainable weight loss, according to research published in *Appetite*.[8]

---

[7]L. Fontana, and Klein, S. (2007), Aging, Adiposity, and Calorie Restriction, *The Journal of the American Medical Association* (often cross-referenced in J. Nutr.).

[8]B. Wansink, & Painter, J.E. (2007), 'The mindless margin and the 20% solution', *Appetite*, *49*(1), p. 328

Feel-Good Hormones

The Hidden Benefit: when you eat with intention and stop before fullness, your body rewards you:

- Serotonin levels rise as breath helps modulate this neurotransmitter, many of which are produced in the gut
- Dopamine is released when you feel in control, helping reduce cravings
- Endorphins increase through small acts of self-care

You leave the table energized, not heavy. Lightness becomes your new joy.

Real-Life Case Study

From Overeating to Empowerment

Ria, a 39-year-old PR consultant, ate clean—salads, soups, no sugar—yet constantly felt bloated and fatigued. Her issue wasn't what she ate, but how. Meals were rushed. Portions, excessive. Before the breath practice, Ria would often feel a heavy, dull ache after meals, followed by an inexplicable urge to grab a sugary snack to 'reset'. Her evenings were often spent feeling sluggish. I introduced her to the 7 Breaths Practice, to relax and align with slimming goals before meals.

From Craving to Cues

Adarsh, a 51-year-old content creator, found himself 'hungry' all the time. But it wasn't hunger—it was habit. Late nights, deadlines, high stress, constant snacking. When he started the breath practice before each snack, within two weeks:

- His cravings dropped.

- His snacking was cut in half.
- He reported feeling 'clearer, lighter, and more in control'.

He hadn't changed what he ate. He changed why.

Two months later, he noticed these changes:

- Bloating vanished.
- Energy remained steady.
- Sleep improved.
- He lost weight.

But more importantly, his mindset transformed. Lightness—physical and emotional became his new normal.

Many people tell me, 'I eat so carefully. My diet is perfect.' And I gently ask, 'Then why isn't it working?' Often, we know what to eat. But it's the how—with awareness, rhythm and self-kindness—that creates lasting change.

Tiny Shifts, Big Impact

- Stop before you're full.
- Breathe before you begin.
- Allow space to digest, reflect, reset.

These small actions build powerful momentum, connecting mind, body and spirit in the most nourishing way. They directly optimize the gut-brain conversation, ensuring your internal signals are clear and responsive.

Gentle Tools to Shift from Fullness to Lightness

When cravings strike or old habits resurface, try:

- Sipping warm cinnamon tea, a turmeric latte or milk (almond, soy, oat, or regular)

- Brewing a cup of peppermint or fennel tea
- Rinsing your mouth or brushing your teeth
- Journalling with the prompt: 'Am I really hungry?'
- Simply stepping away from the table or the kitchen
- Taking a few slow, grounding breaths before reaching for something

These small rituals can softly anchor you in your body and the now. Experiment with them, and notice how your body and mind respond. Your journey to lightness isn't a race—it's a discovery, made one conscious choice at a time. You won't always get it 'right'—and that's okay. The goal isn't perfection, but presence. Each small pause is an act of self-care.

NamitaSpeaks

The 7 Breaths Practice (≈ 1 minute) and the Mini Breath practice (≈ 30 seconds) are portable, powerful and simple. They're not just slimming tools. They are doorways to calm, clarity and conscious living. When you tune in to breath and awareness, eating becomes more than a routine. It becomes healing.

3

Mental Mastery from the Masters: Inspired by Sport Psychology, Martial Arts and Monks

What do a Grand Slam tennis champion, a black belt martial artist and a meditating monk have in common?

It's not a trick question. The answer lies at the heart of 7 Breaths to Slimming—a simple yet powerful method that goes far beyond weight loss. It's a journey into mental mastery.

When I first introduced the 7 Breaths Practice, I focused mainly on how it works—the steps, the technique, the outcomes. But I didn't share enough about what inspired it.

This approach was shaped by years of observing excellence up close. I've seen top athletes enter high-stakes moments with unwavering focus—like a tennis champion taking a deep, grounding breath before serving at match point, letting the world fade away for that single swing. I've watched martial artists move with silent strength and presence. And I've sat with monks who radiate calm and clarity. Despite their differences, they all share one thing: profound mastery over the mind.

And that's what this method is truly about—not restriction, but self-awareness, discipline and inner strength.

The good news? You don't need years of training in a dojo or a monastery to access this kind of mental power. The same mindset that fuels their performance can transform your relationship with food, your body and yourself.

Because whether it's sports, martial arts, or your own slimming journey—success starts in the mind. 7 Breaths to Slimming simplifies this powerful truth, making it accessible and achievable for anyone, every single day.

The Athlete's Edge: Visualisation, Focus and Ritual

In high-level sport, success isn't solely the result of physical training. It's built on mental resilience. Athletes visualize every move, stay composed under pressure and commit to consistent routines that shape their peak performance. Just as they 'pre-pave' their success through mental rehearsal, your breath practice allows you to mentally prepare for your meal, setting the intention with clarity and control—even before the first bite.

This same mindset lies at the heart of lasting health and wellness. The 7 Breaths technique is rooted in that very principle—guiding you to cultivate discipline and focus before eating. By training the breath, you train the mind. Each conscious pause becomes a moment of empowered control, helping you approach food with clarity and purpose.

Over time, this simple practice becomes the foundation for sustainable weight loss. It's the consistent application of breath that strengthens the neural pathways for effortless discipline—transforming intention into habit.

Remember, it's not about perfection. It's about practice. Every conscious breath rewires the brain, reinforcing your ability to eat with awareness until it becomes second nature.

Dr Dinshaw Pardiwala, renowned orthopaedic surgeon who works with Olympic athletes and Indian cricketers, echoes this philosophy: '*As Namita highlights in this book, discipline is the invisible foundation of lasting success. Whether it's showing up for rehab, staying mentally focused, committing to recovery routines, or even to slimming goals—consistent discipline transforms potential into achievement.*'

The path to slimming is grounded in focus and mental control. That's why this isn't just breathwork—it's a mental reset. It trains your mind to pause, reflect and then act. This approach transcends rigid external diet rules, fostering an internal compass that intuitively aligns with your body's real needs.

When I asked **Mohammad Azharuddin, the legendary batsman and former captain of the Indian cricket team, about his rigorous cricket training and its connection to slimming for health, he shared:** '*Focus and discipline are key—whether in cricket or health. Just like a batsman composes himself between deliveries, 7 Breaths trains the mind for portion control. I commend Namita for this game-changing approach to weight loss.*'

You might not be facing a fast bowler or climbing a mountain, but you face your own daily challenges—a tempting snack, a stressful meal or simply the automatic habit of eating. The beauty of this breath practice is how it distils grand principles of mental mastery into a practical, accessible tool for everyday life.

Martial Arts: The Discipline of Stillness in Motion

This philosophy aligns deeply with the ancient wisdom of martial arts—whether it's karate in Japan, tai chi in China, kalaripayattu in Kerala, or gatka among Sikh warriors.

Kung Fu, often misunderstood as merely combat, literally means 'skill achieved through hard work and time'. It reflects the idea that mastery—of movement, mind, or even mindful eating—is the result of discipline and deliberate practice.

Across traditions, students are taught that movement begins not with action, but with stillness. Breath comes first, then intention, then motion. As one martial saying goes: 'The fight is won before it begins.' Victory comes not from aggression, but from preparedness, presence and control.

Another guiding phrase: 'One breath, one mind, one move.' This speaks to the integration of body, breath and thought—the very principle 7 Breaths embraces. Before each meal, each craving, each decision you pause. You centre yourself. You respond and not react.

Micro-practice: The next time a craving hits, instead of immediately reaching for food, pause for the Mini Breath practice. Visualize yourself making a calm, conscious choice, just like a master prepares for their next move.

Interesting fact: Martial arts masters train in Mushin—a Zen concept meaning 'no mind'. In this state, the mind is free from fear, anger or ego—allowing the body to move fluidly and instinctively. It's the same state athletes call 'the zone', and the same presence we cultivate with each focused breath.

In traditional samurai training, warriors practised kiai—a powerful shout that channels breath and energy into a single moment. It wasn't just about strength—it synchronized mind and body into pure focus. Kalaripayattu uses a similar alignment of breath, movement and energy in its flowing sequences.

Monastic Wisdom: Mastery through Breath

Even more inspiring are the monks who train not in gyms or dojos, but in the quiet temples of the mind. Their daily discipline is the breath itself. To sit in silence, to observe without judgement, to detach from desire—this is their practice.

In Zen Buddhism, focused breathing is central to meditation. Similarly, in ancient Indian yogic tradition, pranayama (breath control) is the bridge between the body and the soul. Sage Patanjali wrote that through conscious breath, we attain mastery over thought and emotion.

One popular Zen quote reminds us: 'You should sit in meditation for 20 minutes a day. Unless you're too busy—then sit for an hour.' This paradox points to a deeper truth: when life feels out of control, don't speed up—slow down.

Monks don't resist desire—they transcend it. They know control doesn't come from force, but from focus. Indian yogis speak of *vairagya* (detachment) and *dhyana* (meditation) as paths to balanced living.

Across spiritual traditions around the world, synchronized breath and intention are used to align with deeper goals. Whether in prayer, meditation or stillness, the breath is a tool for connection—both within and beyond.

NamitaSpeaks

Whether it's the calculated calm of an athlete, the focused readiness of a martial artist or the centred stillness of a monk, the lesson is the same: when you train your breath, you train your mind. When you train your mind, you transform your life. One breath. One pause. One conscious choice at a time. Embrace your inner master. The power to transform your life, bite by conscious bite, is literally at your fingertips—or rather, in your breath.

4

Wellness Retreats: Carry It Home

There's something magical about stepping away from life's constant buzz—alarms, alerts, meetings and meals on the go. From spa breaks and wellness retreats to naturopathy centres, Ayurvedic therapies and detox getaways, we're spoiled for choice when it comes to taking a wellness pause. While these experiences often require time, commitment and planning, they offer invaluable opportunities for rest, reflection and a deep reset.

They offer powerful recalibrations—a bubble where balance is restored and clarity returns. Surrounded by nature, nourished by healing meals, treatments and holistic practices, you begin to feel lighter, clearer and more connected to your body and self. Some leave feeling recharged, others, uncertain.

However, regardless of the outcome, the true journey begins once you return to everyday life, where the supportive environment disappears, routines slip away and daily demands take over. Suddenly, you're juggling deadlines, navigating tempting office snacks, managing social pressures at dinner parties or simply struggling to find time to prep a healthy meal. Without a daily anchor, the clarity and momentum you worked so hard to build can begin to fade.

Your Everyday Reset

This is where your breath becomes your most accessible ally. The 7 Breaths Practice—seven deep, mindful breaths taken slowly in about a minute—is a simple yet powerful ritual that keeps you rooted in the calm, clarity and commitment you cultivated during your retreat. It acts as an immediate stress antidote, lowering cortisol levels and preventing reactive eating patterns that daily pressures often trigger. The practice carries those benefits into everyday life, supporting sustainable slimming and balance, without stress or extremes.

Each conscious breath is a quiet act of return. Over time, these small moments accumulate, leading to effortless and lasting results. These micro-habits, consistently applied, create macro-changes, building resilience that lasts. It's a powerful tool for mindful integration, allowing you to weave healthy patterns into your busy life naturally, rather than treating them as another chore.

Slimming isn't a retreat result—it's a daily rhythm, shaped by breath and choice. Everyone's path is unique, even when following the same diet or regimen. Genetics, metabolism, habits and emotional triggers all play a role, making slimming a deeply personal and ongoing process. That's why retreat time should feel inspiring and enjoyable, not like a boot camp.

When the experience becomes too rigid or punishing, weight often rebounds, sometimes even more than before. Most retreats follow structured seven-, fourteen- or twenty-one-day programs, with curated meals, exercise, detox protocols and close supervision. In that environment, discipline feels easier, and results often follow. But once you're home, those habits are challenged. While some maintain momentum, others struggle.

This is where self-compassion is key. Breath practice isn't about perfection—it's a gentle, non-judgemental invitation to return to your intentional path, even after a stumble. True transformation is sustainable, and not just inside the retreat but beyond it.

Common Challenges and How Breath Practice Helps

After returning home, the journey isn't without obstacles. Stress, social temptations, fatigue, travel and emotional ups and downs can challenge your best intentions. Breath practice offers a simple yet powerful way to navigate these moments:

- Stress and Overwhelm: Calms your nervous system and breaks the cycle of emotional eating.
- Social Situations: Creates a pause to choose consciously, rather than react impulsively.
- Fatigue and Low Energy: Boosts oxygen flow and supports a clearer, more focused mind.
- Travel and Routine Disruptions: Anchors you with a portable ritual that restores balance anywhere.
- Emotional Ups and Downs: Grounds you gently with self-compassion and presence, guiding you back to your goals.

Anchor Your Retreat Gains

A retreat can leave you feeling lighter, recharged, and deeply motivated. But how do you hold on to those gains once you're back in the flow of daily life? The real transformation begins when you bring small, sustainable habits home.

Here's how the 7 Breaths Practice (about one minute) and the Mini Breath practice (around thirty seconds) can support you:

How the Breath Practice Supports You

1. **7 Breaths Practice before Meals:** This simple pause reconnects you to your body. It naturally supports portion control and encourages slower, more conscious eating. Rina, a yoga teacher from Pune, shared: 'When I do the 7 Breaths, I eat slower and stop at eighty per cent fullness—without guilt or rules.'
2. **Use the Mini Breath When Cravings Hit:** In just thirty seconds, the Mini Breath helps you pause during stress or boredom-induced cravings. Liam, an advertising executive from Sydney, said: 'It helps me pause just long enough to ask—am I hungry, or just triggered?'
3. **Sunday Evenings—a Breath Ritual for Balance:** Dedicate this time to check in and reset your rhythm. Roshni, a working mom from Bengaluru, shared: 'Now I start Sunday evenings with the 7 Breaths Practice before dinner. It tames my weekend binge and gently sets the tone for the week—it feels like self-care, not control.'
4. **Make Breath Part of Your Meal Routine Anywhere:** Just like washing your hands before eating, pre-meal breath becomes a quiet, consistent ritual. Whether at a restaurant, buffet, dinner party or quick lunch, it's your invisible anchor, enhancing digestion and awareness.
5. **Proactive Breathing in Tempting Situations:** Before entering a buffet, dinner party or office pantry, try the Mini Breath practice. It builds a subtle shield of awareness.

Daily Breath Practice Checklist

- Do 7 Breaths before at least one meal a day.
- Try the Mini Breath practice when cravings strike.
- Anchor Sunday evenings with a reset breath.
- Use a breath pause at social gatherings.
- Keep it gentle. Keep it going.

The retreat may end, but your breath carries the reset home.

Real-Life Reflections

Participants from an online workshop on breath practice shared how these tools helped sustain slimming and inner balance after their wellness retreats:

Sonal, Delhi: Breathe and Transform: *'After my 14-day detox in Bali, I worried about slipping back into old habits. Then I remembered your 7 Breaths Practice. Committing to it before lunch and dinner helped me stay grounded and avoid overeating.'*
Takeaway: Breathwork created a simple anchor to maintain detox gains back home.

Nicolas, Melbourne: Mini Breath, Major Impact: *'I used to struggle with late-night snacking. Now, I do the Mini Breath, and it stops me from mindless munching. It's a small change that transformed my habits.'*
Takeaway: *A thirty-second breath replaced night time snacking with a mindful pause.*

Rajesh, regional sales manager: On-the-Go Clarity: *'My work involves constant travel and client dinners, which used to be diet death traps. But after learning the Mini Breath, I now use it discreetly before every meal out. It helps me choose wisely*

and stop before overeating, even when everyone else is still going. It's truly portable peace of mind.'
Takeaway: Breath practice helped navigate social eating and regain control, without restriction.

Meera, Thailand: From Spa to City: *'During my wellness retreat in Koh Samui, the spa routine was amazing, but what stayed with me was your Mini Breath. Back in Bangkok, I use it before every meal. It's my anchor in the chaos of work.'*
Takeaway: A simple breath practice became a daily reset tool in a high-stress job.

Elena, Switzerland: Structured to Self-Guided: *'I attended a detox program in the Swiss Alps with every detail meticulously planned. But once home, it was your 7 Breaths Practice that helped me stay centred. Now, it's my go-to pre-meal ritual—calming and effective.'*
Takeaway: The breath ritual turned a structured retreat habit into a personal daily anchor.

Claire, New York: Big City, Small Pause: *'At an Ayurvedic spa in Kerala, I reconnected with my body through therapies and nourishing food. But it was your 7 Breaths Practice that created a lasting shift. Even now, back in New York, I begin every meal with those seven breaths—it's my moment of pause and presence.'*
Takeaway: Breathwork bridged the gap between retreat clarity and city-life stress.

Frequently Asked Questions

Q: Can breath practice replace other wellness activities, such as exercise or healthy eating?
A: Breath practice is a powerful complement, not a substitute.

It reduces stress and enhances awareness, helping you stay disciplined with food and lifestyle choices.

Q: Is breath practice suitable for everyone?

A: Yes! It's gentle and appropriate for all ages, fitness levels and lifestyles.

Q: How can I stay motivated to keep practising daily?

A: Anchor your practice to everyday moments—before meals, during commutes or as part of your evening routine. Think of it as an act of self-kindness, not just another task. Celebrate small wins—they build momentum and lead to lasting change.

NamitaSpeaks

Gentle yet powerful, your breath keeps you connected to your goals, wherever life takes you. So yes, enjoy your retreat. Soak in the calm, the nourishment, the lightness. But above all, don't forget your breath. It's the simplest, most potent ritual you carry with you—delivering lasting transformation long after your break ends. This isn't just about finishing a retreat—it's about transforming how you live. With every conscious breath, you reclaim your calm, your clarity and your commitment. Let your breath be the wellness practice that never ends.

5

Slimming in the Age of Speed: Why You Still Need Discipline

In today's fast-paced world, where instant results are expected and solutions come in injections, surgeries and machines, it's tempting to believe transformation can be outsourced. For many, these options offer convenience; for others, they represent a last resort—a desperate hope after years of struggle, promising a swift escape from the emotional and physical burden of excess weight. But even the most advanced interventions—whether medically necessary like bariatric surgery or chosen for ease require something timeless for lasting success: presence and discipline.

As **Dr Shashank Shah, a leading bariatric surgeon**, puts it: '*"7 Breaths to Slimming" is a powerful pre-meal reminder. As Namita shares, this simple breath practice helps patients pause, refocus and stop at just enough—an essential habit for sustaining results after bariatric surgery.*'

It's important to acknowledge that for those facing severe obesity and health complications, bariatric surgery can be life-saving. It triggers significant physiological changes and often provides a much-needed kickstart to better health. But this chapter isn't just about different weight-loss approaches, it is about the mindset needed to sustain them. Whether surgery, medication or lifestyle change, true transformation demands more than following a plan. It requires ongoing commitment, self-awareness and inner alignment.

Transformation is rarely a straight path. There will be setbacks, temptations and times when giving up feels easier. But it's in these very moments that discipline transforms—from a routine into a quiet promise to yourself. A commitment to keep going, even when progress feels invisible. Even medically guided interventions—often mistaken as quick fixes—demand consistent effort and require deep, consistent effort for lasting changes.

Take a closer look at any success story of athletes, musicians, spiritual masters or business leaders—and you'll see it's never just luck or hacks. It's the steady power of discipline and focus.

Yes, we live in an age of rapid advancements—AI, biohacking, slimming apps, metabolic boosters. Technology has changed the game, but it can't replace the human grit needed for sustainable results. The message is simple: Discipline isn't outdated. It's irreplaceable.

The Shortcut Boom: Do They Deliver Long-Term?

We live in an era where weight loss has taken a high-tech turn—from appetite-suppressing injections to non-invasive machines promising inch loss, from surgeries to personalized metabolic boosters—there's something for every goal, budget and body type. But here's the catch: are these options truly sustainable? And do they come with hidden clauses?

Take Maya, a thirty-five-year-old music teacher, for example. She tried a popular fat-burning device and was thrilled when inches seemed to melt away in just a few weeks. Excited by the results, she felt motivated—until her usual eating patterns and sedentary habits crept back in. Within months, the inches returned, reminding her that shortcuts rarely replace consistent, mindful lifestyle habits.

This isn't about promoting or dismissing any method. It's about recognizing a reality we can't ignore. Today, weight loss isn't just a personal journey—it's a booming industry, powered by social media, the idealization of 'perfect' bodies and the relentless demand for quick results.

Each year brings a flood of new options—promising, scientific, seductive. But it's essential to approach them informed. Marketing highlights immediate results while often downplaying the absolute necessity of sustained behavioural change and internal discipline.

Choosing the right path is deeply personal and ideally guided by qualified professionals. Always seek advice from board-certified, reputable doctors who understand your unique health profile. Because the real question isn't: 'Which shortcut is best?' It's: 'Which path is realistic and supports my long-term well-being?'

In the noise of quick fixes and shortcuts, this breath practice offers a return to basics—presence, pause and inner alignment. Because lasting transformation begins with a single breath, a conscious choice and the discipline to honour it every day.

Mind over Matter: The Mental Side of Slimming

Weight loss isn't just about calories or procedures—it's a deeply mental journey. Our brains seek comfort, reward and safety—often through food. Emotional eating, stress responses and old habits can derail even the best intentions. That's why training the mind is essential.

The breath practice in this book offers a simple yet

powerful technique: a pause between impulse and action—a space where real choice becomes possible. It's in that pause that discipline shifts from a rigid rule to a personal habit. That's why it's designed as a pre-meal practice—to help you feel centred, in control and more intentional about what follows.

Repeated conscious choices build new neural pathways, making healthy behaviours feel natural over time. When the mind learns to distinguish true hunger from emotional triggers, eating becomes nourishment, not escape. This is especially vital after procedures, when the body changes, but mental habits remain.

The body may transform, but it's the mind that sustains. Look closely at lasting weight-loss success stories, and you'll find a hidden strength: mental resilience. The ability to stay focused, manage stress and bounce back from setbacks doesn't just support physical change—it anchors it.

Even when interventions provide a physical reset, the breath practice guides the mind toward powerful non-scale victories:

- Renewed energy to power your day
- Restful sleep that resets your metabolism
- Mental clarity that sharpens your focus

These crucial changes power sustainable slimming success.

Case Studies: From Shortcuts to Sustainability

Radhika: From Injections to Inner Connection

At 38, Radhika turned to weekly weight-loss injections after years of post-pregnancy struggles. She dropped nine kilos in three months and felt unstoppable—until the weight returned in unexpected places once the injections stopped. 'It wasn't just the physical change—it was the panic of losing control,' she said. Through a wellness workshop, she discovered the 7 Breaths Practice and began using it before meals. 'It brought me back into my body,' she shared. 'I started responding to real needs instead of reacting to cravings.' Her weight loss slowed but became sustainable and empowering.

Arjun: The Liposuction Wake-Up Call

At 45, Arjun turned to abdominal liposuction to undo years of sedentary living. The results were instant—four inches gone. But without real lifestyle changes, the fat returned within months. 'I thought surgery was the solution,' he admits. 'But it should have been the starting point.' Working with a coach, Arjun adopted the breath practice and gradually built discipline around his meals. As Arjun explains, 'Just that pause helped me think before eating. It's something I'll follow for life.'

Sanjay: The Bariatric Breakthrough

At 51, Sanjay underwent bariatric surgery for obesity-related issues. While he lost twenty kilos in a year, his mental habits remained unchanged. 'I still craved junk—I just couldn't eat as much,' he admitted. His dietician suggested incorporating the breath practice. 'That changed everything. It helped me eat intentionally instead of emotionally,' Sanjay remarked. Today, Sanjay maintains his weight through self-awareness, routine and a renewed mindset.

Nisha: From Machines to Mindfulness

At 29, Nisha used non-invasive inch-loss machines to slim down before a wedding. 'It worked—but only temporarily,' she said. She later joined a wellness group and discovered the breath practice. 'I stopped eating mindlessly. I became more aware—not just of food, but of what I was feeling before I reached for it.' The machine shaped her body temporarily. The breath practice reshaped her relationship with food.

5 Smart Questions to Ask before Choosing a Weight-Loss Procedure

1. Is it permanent or temporary? Understand the timeline. Many interventions deliver short-term change but require long-term lifestyle shifts to sustain the results.
2. What are the side effects, both common and rare? Don't stop at the brochure. Ask for real-world data and long-term outcomes—not just the highlights.
3. What happens when I stop? Whether it's injections, machines or medication—what's your exit plan? Know what to expect once the support is removed.
4. How will I maintain the results? Think beyond the procedure. What's your strategy for sleep, stress, movement and controlled eating?
5. Who is guiding me? Choose credibility over convenience. Look for qualified, board-certified professionals—and never settle for a one-size-fits-all promise.

The Discipline Principle

Technology can jumpstart your journey. Medical interventions—like surgery or medication—can offer valuable support. But the breath practice is what brings it all together. It's not a replacement, but a vital companion to any approach, helping you build the mental strength and self-awareness that make change last.

Because here's the reality: no tool, however advanced, can create consistency for you.

That comes from within, through daily habits, conscious choices and inner alignment. Without discipline, even the most promising methods can fall short. With it, progress becomes sustainable—and truly yours.

As outlined earlier, the breath practice is more than a calming ritual—it's a focused sequence designed to move you from impulse to intention. Breaths one and two ground you in calm; breaths three to five awaken your inner strength; and breaths six and seven seal your commitment.

Each breath acts as a micro-intervention, moving you from reaction to conscious control. Focus. Daily choices. Accountability. These are the threads that hold your efforts together, especially when quick fixes start to fray.

Because here's the truth behind every trend: shortcuts may open doors, but only discipline walks you through—and helps you stay.

NamitaSpeaks

Whether it's injections, machines or surgery, every shortcut can play a role in a weight-loss journey. But no device, drug or high-tech fix can replace what truly sustains transformation: discipline, self-awareness and emotional connection.

The breath practice isn't a miracle cure—it's a simple pause, a gateway back to your body's wisdom—the cues that technology often drowns out. Yes, the body may transform, but it's the mind that sustains. In the race for instant results, it's tempting to outsource transformation. But real, lasting change begins in a quieter space—where you choose presence over impulse, discipline over shortcuts. That's the space where transformation takes root—and becomes your own.

6

Your Questions, Answered

It's completely natural to have questions when trying something new, especially when it comes to slimming, habits, and well-being. The 7 Breaths Practice isn't a diet or a quick fix. It's a gentle, empowering pause before meals—a simple breathing method that can transform how you relate to food, emotions and yourself.

Rooted in science and shaped by real-life experience, this practice helps you tune in to your body's true needs and feel more in control, without restriction or pressure.

Here are the most common questions I receive, answered with care to support you on your journey toward balanced, joyful and sustainable living:

1. **'7 Breaths to Slimming'—doesn't that suggest an aspiration to be slim? Isn't that a form of body shaming?**
   Not at all. In this book, 'slimming' is about personal choice, not pressure. If you're content with your body, there's no need to change it. This isn't about linking worth to weight. Confidence stands strong at any size. The message is simple: self-esteem isn't conditional—it's your constant.
2. **Can this method help with weight loss?**
   Yes, because it changes your relationship with food.

Over time, your appetite adjusts, your stomach adapts and your decisions align with your body's real needs. When intention leads the way, eating with care becomes a habit. Weight loss often follows naturally, not forcefully.

3. **How quickly will I see results?**
   This journey isn't about instant fixes—it's about lasting transformation. Many people notice improved digestion and greater self-awareness early on. Visible changes in weight or deeply rooted habits vary from person to person. For some, shifts show within days, for others, it may take weeks. It depends on your consistency, commitment and mindset. Progress looks different for everyone. What matters most is that you're moving forward.
4. **How do I monitor fullness and stop eating at eighty per cent?**
   Think of eighty per cent as a comfortable stopping point. It's not about rules—it's about rhythm. You feel nourished, not stuffed. The breath helps you slow down enough to notice that moment, so meals leave you feeling light, not heavy.
5. **What about exercise—shouldn't that be part of any weight-loss journey?**
   Absolutely. Exercise is essential for health, energy and long-term weight balance. This practice isn't a replacement—it's one piece of the puzzle. Aligning your intention before eating helps reinforce your efforts across the board.
6. **Can I do this if I have a medical condition like diabetes or thyroid issues?**
   Yes. The practice supports digestion, reduces stress

and encourages balance—all of which help in managing chronic conditions. However, it's important to consult your doctor for personalized advice before starting.

7. **Can I still enjoy my favourite foods? Can I feel satisfied with smaller portions?**
   Can I use this practice before snacks too? Of course. This isn't about giving up pleasure—it's about knowing when to stop. When you eat in a calm state, fullness cues emerge naturally. You can use this practice before meals or snacks to savour without slipping into excess.
8. **Will this help with emotional eating and cravings?**
   Yes. The breath creates a pause between feeling and action. That gap gives you space to respond, not react.
9. **Can this help reduce bloating and digestive discomfort?**
   Yes. Breathing deeply before meals shifts your body into a relaxed state, supporting digestion and reducing bloating.
10. **Will this work if I have a slow metabolism or hormonal issues?**
    Yes. It reduces cortisol and eases stress, both of which affect appetite and hormonal balance.
11. **What if I'm too busy for the full practice?**
    Try the Mini Breath practice—the final three breaths of the full practice. It creates a powerful shift before meals or snacks—even on the go.
12. **What if I forget to do the practice?**
    That's completely normal! Don't let a missed moment turn into a missed day. Just return to your breath practice at your next meal or snack. Each moment

is a fresh chance to begin again—with purpose and without self-criticism.

13. **Does this help even if I eat at my desk or on the go?**
Yes. Even a short pause, like the Mini Breath practice, helps your body prepare for food, no matter where you are.
14. **How can I stay consistent?**
Link the practice to mealtimes. Set gentle reminders or use visual cues. With repetition, it becomes a comforting part of your daily rhythm.
15. **Can children or elderly people use this method?**
Yes. It's a safe and calming practice for all ages. It supports digestion, emotional regulation and a more peaceful relationship with food.
16. **Can I do this in public or at restaurants?**
Yes. A few quiet breaths can be done discreetly—no one even needs to know.
17. **Will I feel more in control of my eating?**
Yes. Over time, you'll shift from impulsive patterns to conscious, empowered choices.
18. **What if I overeat even after doing the practice?**
Be kind to yourself. This isn't about perfection—it's about progress. Each breath is a chance to reset.
19. **Can it help with binge eating?**
It can help create space, but if binge eating is frequent, professional support is important. This practice can be a valuable part of healing.
20. **Can I use this during intermittent fasting?**
Yes. It complements fasting beautifully, helping you return to food with presence and balance.
21. **Is there science behind this?**
Yes. Breathwork is proven to reduce cortisol, activate

the parasympathetic nervous system and support digestion and emotional regulation.[9]

22. **How does this help me truly trust my body's signals?**
By consistently creating that pause before eating, you begin to distinguish between true physiological hunger and other triggers like emotions or habits. Over time, this conscious listening rebuilds your body's innate wisdom, allowing you to intuitively eat what you need, when you need it, and stop when you're truly nourished—freeing you from relying on external rules.

23. **What if others around me don't do it?**
That's okay. This is your moment. Your calm might quietly inspire others.

24. **What if friends or family try to discourage or sabotage my new habits?**
It's common for loved ones to inadvertently challenge new routines, often out of their own comfort zone or misunderstanding. Remember, this practice is for your well-being. Gently explain your intention if you feel comfortable or simply focus on your breath without seeking approval. Your consistency and positive changes will speak volumes over time.

25. **How does this compare to mindful eating apps or other techniques?**
Many tools offer valuable support, and you can certainly use them along with this practice. The unique power of the breath practice lies in its absolute simplicity, portability and zero-cost accessibility. It

---

[9]Siebieszuk, Anna, et al., 'Breathwork for Chronic Stress and Mental Health: Does Choosing a Specific Technique Matter?', *Medical Sciences (Basel)*, Vol. 13, No. 3, Article. 127, 2025.

strips away complexity, bringing you back to the most fundamental and always-available tool: your own breath.

26. **Can I add affirmations or gratitude to the practice?**
    Absolutely. A few words of appreciation or intention can enrich the experience.
27. **When's the best time to start?**
    Now. Don't wait for the perfect moment—start with your next meal. One breath, one bite at a time.
28. **Why haven't you included other important elements like sleep, eating slowly or chewing well?**
    To keep things focused and manageable, this book centres on one powerful habit: pause, breathe, and stop at eighty percent. Once this practice becomes natural, other healthy behaviours—like better sleep, mindful eating pace and thorough chewing—often fall into place on their own. Keeping it simple allows the change to feel achievable and sustainable. Let this practice be your foundation and watch the rest follow.

NamitaSpeaks

Your breath is always with you—free, gentle and deeply powerful. Let this small but mighty practice guide you toward a life of greater calm, connection and care. Breathe before you bite and let the transformation unfold, one meal at a time. This simple breath—your constant companion—is all you need to master your plate and embrace innate balance.

SECTION FIVE

The Future of Slimming: The Path Forward

Welcome to a new era of effortless transformation. This section invites you to explore how a simple yet profound practice—anchored in breath and intention—can lead to lasting change. By integrating ancient wisdom with the pace of modern life, the journey becomes less about restriction and more about reconnection.

Through inspiring global voices, you'll witness how real people, from all walks of life, are quietly reshaping their relationship with food and with themselves—proving that sustainable weight loss is truly within reach, one conscious breath at a time.

1

The New Era: Breath, Intention and Quiet Change

Step into a new era of effortless weight loss.

7 Breaths to Slimming isn't just another method—it's a quiet revolution.

Backed by science, rooted in simplicity, it brings lasting change without struggle. Imagine eating less, feeling more satisfied and releasing excess, not through restriction, but through presence. This conscious presence is what makes sustainable weight loss feel truly effortless, transforming struggle into flow.

This is freedom from food battles.

Not control, but awareness.

Not restriction—but consistent practice.

'Feelings come and go like clouds in a windy sky. Conscious breathing is my anchor.'

—Thich Nhat Hanh

Before I shared 7 Breaths to Slimming with the world, before conducting seminars or workshops, I tried it on myself. I needed to experience it to know it brought peace, not pressure.

Here's what I discovered.

Despite all technology, trackers, apps and smart plans, lasting change still comes back to one timeless principle: awareness. I searched everywhere—books, diets, programmes—looking for answers. But the truth was always with me, in every breath I took.

In today's 'fast-fix' culture, we're surrounded by quick fixes: wearables like smartwatches, fitness bands and health rings track every move, heartbeat and breath. Nutrition apps count every calorie. Even appetite suppressants promise instant results.

These tools may offer quick fixes, but they often bypass deeper transformation. 7 Breaths to Slimming works alongside technology, but it brings awareness to the forefront. It invites you to reconnect with what's always been within: your breath.

Technology and Tradition: A New Balance

In an age of hyperconnectivity, simplicity is making a powerful comeback:

- Wearables show signs of stress—your breath gives you the power to shift it.
- Apps can guide meals—your breath aligns your mindset.
- Medications may suppress appetite—your breath cultivates presence.

Let Technology Support and Not Distract.

Even one conscious breath between meetings or in traffic can centre you. Set a digital reminder if needed. Let technology assist you, not overwhelm your journey. This integration of timeless wisdom with modern living marks a holistic approach, where inner alignment guides every choice.

The Emotional Gateway: Breathe Before You Eat

We often eat from emotion, not hunger. Stress. Boredom. Loneliness.

> Breath meets emotion at the door.
> Inhale.
> Exhale.
> Shift.
> You move from reacting…to responding.

Real Stories, Real Shifts

Ravi's Story: Guilt to Gratitude

Ravi always viewed food as the enemy. He tried everything from fasting to dieting to overexercising. Then suddenly, he traced back to the idea of 7 Breaths to Slimming, which he had come across during a seminar on 'Good Living'. He decided to give the 7 Breaths Practice a shot. When he began pairing breathwork with affirmations before meals and committed to the 7 Breaths Practice, his relationship with food began to shift. He lost weight—yes, that is right, but more importantly, he gained focus and peace. Mindless eating became mindful moments. Guilt dissolved into gratitude.

Anjali's Shift: From Craving to Calm

Anjali once stood in front of the fridge, craving a slice of cake, not from hunger, but from frustration after a stressful call.

She paused. She remembered the 7 Breaths Practice from a workshop at her workplace, and she thought to herself, just seven breaths.

Each inhale softened the tension. Each exhale eased the craving. She closed the fridge, not in resistance, but in peace. A small moment. A powerful breakthrough.

These stories aren't exceptions. They're real possibilities—and they're waiting for you, too.

Create Your Ritual

As you deepen your consistency with the 7 Breaths, you may want to explore these complementary practices. They share the core principle of internal alignment and can further enhance your journey toward holistic well-being:

- Tapping (EFT): Emotional Freedom Technique (EFT) uses gentle tapping on specific acupressure points to calm the nervous system and reduce emotional stress. Emotional Freedom Techniques (EFT), also known as tapping, is a self-help method for reducing stress and negative emotions by tapping on specific acupressure points on the face and body while focusing on a problem.
- Brainwave Entrainment: Uses sound frequencies to shift mental state
- Sound Healing: Vibrations to reset energy and emotion
- Visualization: Picture your goal and align action with vision
- Mantras and Chanting: Evoke inner stillness through sacred sound
- Guided Meditations: Gentle prompts to tune in to your body

- Movement Rituals: Stretches or mindful walks
- Journalling: Reflect, release, and stay intentional
- Grounding with Nature: Reconnect with the earth for clarity
- Digital Breath Reminders: Tech as an anchor, not a distraction

Gentle Reminders for Real Life

Life gets busy. You may forget. That's okay.

- Missed your 7 Breaths before a meal? Begin again—no guilt, no drama.
- Too rushed for a full practice? Try the Mini Breath practice as suggested in this book.
- Feeling overwhelmed? Let your breath be the one thing you return to.

Consistency—not perfection—is what counts.

NamitaSpeaks

Breathe Into a New You.
Pause—not to do more, but to feel more.
Notice your breath. Feel the quiet shift.
This isn't the end. It's the beginning of something real, sustainable and yours.
Trust it and watch yourself transform.

2

Global Voices: Real Experiences with 7 Breaths to Slimming

Life rarely unfolds in stillness. It's more like a test match, full of chaos, celebration, cravings and the occasional unexpected googly. It's in the midst of that beautiful mess that the 7 Breaths to Slimming practice reveals its quiet strength.

Whether it's the full 7 Breaths or the quick Mini Breath, this is not a practice of perfection. It doesn't ask you to pause your life. It simply moves with you, anchoring you in the very moments you're most likely to drift away from your body, your signals and your goals.

This simple act of focused breathing becomes your built-in pause:

A reset before meals.
A return to intention.
A way to eat with awareness, not from habit or emotion.

Across workshops, wellness retreats, cities, villages and screens, I've seen how breath becomes an integral part of daily life.

It meets people where they are, gently guiding them forward. It honours their intuitive understanding of foods that suit their needs, culture and preferences. From bustling metropolises to quiet homes across continents, these are just a few examples of how people, irrespective of their culture or circumstance, have found an anchor in their breath.

The stories that follow are shared not for applause, but to light a path. They are reminders that transformation doesn't need to be loud or dramatic.

Just breath by breath—you shift.
Just breath by breath—you align.
And slowly, something deep begins to change.
The world is breathing with you.

Real People, Real Shifts

These are everyday voices, each distinct yet united by the steady power of breath.

Teens: The Overwhelmed Student

Lina, 17, São Paulo: Used to skip lunch and binge in the evenings. Stress before exams was often the trigger. Her mom, who had attended a breathwork and intuitive eating workshop, gently introduced Lina to the 7 Breaths Practice. Now, she does the Mini Breath before meals to feel calm and in charge. The evening binges have slowly faded away. 'It's part of my school life now. I eat better, and I feel better,' Lina affirmed.

Kids: From Chaos to Calm

Ken, 12, Tokyo: Practises 7 Breaths after school to move from high energy to calm connection at dinner. His mom says that tantrums have reduced, and so has his evening overeating, especially of sugary treats.

Postpartum: From Exhaustion to Awareness

Nina, Cape Town: Two months postpartum, found herself eating out of fatigue and frustration. The breath practice helped her pause and listen to her needs, not just fill the silence with food.

Holidays: Celebrating without Losing Control

Arjun, London: Used the practice during Christmas feasts. 'I still enjoy dessert, but no more guilt. I eat slower, stop sooner, and feel satisfied with less. I even lost weight without trying,' Arjun explained.

Wellness Retreat: Taking Calm Home

Clara, Bali: Deepened her detox with the 7 Breaths during a spa retreat. She said, 'It changed how I approached food—not just during the retreat, but even now. I eat less but enjoy it more.'

Medical Journey: Grounding through Change

Ahmed, Dubai: Practised the breaths before and after bariatric surgery. He explained, 'It helped with anxiety, digestion and staying grounded. Even my doctor noticed how in control I seemed, especially during recovery.'

Weekend Binge: Reclaiming Sundays

Sofia, New York: Broke the guilt-binge cycle with Sunday night breaths. She remarked of her new routine, 'No more "start again Monday". I just breathe, reset and realign. It's enough.'

Festivals: Savouring the Moment

Aarti, Mumbai: Loves Diwali feasts but used to overeat through the celebrations. 'Now I pause and breathe before meals. I still enjoy everything—I just stop when I've had enough,' she asserted.

Similarly, **Amal, Chennai:** While recovering from surgery, used 7 Breaths during Ramadan. Amal said, 'It helped me read my hunger better and feel more in control during fasting and feasting.'

Shift Workers: Finding Calm in Chaos

Ana, Manila: A night-shift nurse, she says, 'Even on the go, I take three deep breaths before eating. It's helped me cut down on mindless munching during midnight breaks.'

Athletes: Fuelling with Focus

Luca, Rome: A footballer, he uses the breath technique on training days. In his words: 'I was anxious and rushed before. Now, I chew better, eat what I need and stay light for the game.'

Students Abroad: Creating Stability

Mei, Beijing–Toronto: Found comfort in the breaths during her transition to a new country. 'Everything was uncertain. This tiny practice helped me eat with balance—and feel more settled,' Mei said of the breath practice.

Corporate Life: Staying Sharp at the Table

Rajiv, Singapore: 'I used to overeat at client dinners. Now the Mini Breath sets the tone. I pace myself better and walk away feeling clear, not stuffed.'

Emotional Healing: A New Relationship with Food

Sophie, Paris: After a heartbreak, she turned to food for comfort. 'These breaths helped me feel what I was going through—instead of numbing it with food.'

Older Adults: Digesting Life Slowly

Mr Lee, Toronto, 74: 'I eat slower now. I breathe; I chew. My stomach's calmer, and I no longer overeat like before. Even my doctor is happy.'

Family Bonding: Shared Breaths

Fatima, Morocco: Practises the breaths with her daughters before meals. 'It brings us together. We nudge and inspire each other to pause, eat with care and stay committed to our weight goals,' Fatima remarked.

Recovery: Empowering the Body Again

Julia, Melbourne: A stroke survivor, she says, 'I couldn't do much, but I could breathe. That gave me strength. I regained a sense of control, especially around food.'

Eco-Eaters: Conscious Consumption

Daniel, Berlin: A sustainability advocate, he says, 'The breath connects me to my food and my choices. I eat less, waste less and feel more aligned with the planet.'

These diverse stories, spanning age, geography and life's myriad challenges, echo a powerful truth: the capacity for conscious choice and inner calm resides within each of us. Whether navigating a stressful workday, celebrating a holiday or recovering from a major life event, the consistent thread is the profound yet simple power of pausing to breathe.

They remind us that true transformation isn't about escaping life's chaos, but finding your centre within it, where breath becomes the bridge to balance, calm and sustainable slimming.

Reflection Prompt: Your Breath, Your Compass

Let these stories inspire your pause. You don't need perfection—just presence.

Before your next meal, pause and ask:

- What am I truly hungry for?
- Can I be present with my body, right now?
- How do I want to feel after this meal?
- What does nourishment mean to me today?

Let your breath guide you.

You just need a pause.

Because in the pause…clarity returns.

And your relationship with food begins to shift—gently, purposefully and for good.

Takeaway: 7 Breaths to Slimming centres on one essential habit: learning to stop eating at around eighty per cent fullness. Learning to stop at just enough—not quite full—can take a little getting used to. This may feel unfamiliar at first; after all, fullness often feels comforting, especially when it's been a long-held habit.

The breath technique taught in this book becomes a key tool in making this shift. It helps you tune in to your body's true signals, so you can pause and stop before reaching the point of feeling overly full.

It's about finding that 'sweet spot'—a skill that develops gradually with practice.

Over time, this new way of eating becomes second nature, creating space for lightness, renewed energy and lasting change. Breath practice gently supports this transition, making sustainable slimming not just possible, but inevitable.

NamitaSpeaks

7 Breaths to Slimming is a return to self-trust. It moves with you and grows with you. If you fall out of practice, simply begin again. You already have what you need—your breath. This universal tool provides the simplest path to lasting change and sustainable weight loss. Embrace this practice, and discover how calm and empowering your journey to slimming can be when you listen deeply to your body's wisdom.

Conclusion

The Journey Ahead

How many of us truly enjoy stepping out of our comfort zones? Most of us lean towards the familiar; it feels safe, manageable and reassuring. In a world that already demands so much, radically changing our habits can seem overwhelming.

That's why 7 Breaths to Slimming offers a gentler path—a journey that feels more like a steady companion than a disruptive force. As you reach these final pages, I leave you with this thought:

Tune in to your rhythm. Follow your rules.

This breath practice isn't a quick fix. It's a conscious method—grounded in awareness, guided by breath and designed to help you breathe your way into lasting balance and vitality. As you reconnect with your body, slimming unfolds naturally—bringing a sense of ease and harmony.

Make time for the breath practice, and it will always be there for you: steady, grounding and ready to guide you towards your wellness goals and a deeper connection with yourself.

Progress flows from persistence. The more you align your will with your goal, the more energy you awaken within. Remember to meet yourself with kindness and patience on days when consistency feels challenging. This journey is about progress, not perfection.

‘**Pause. Breathe. Align.**’ Just three words, yet they anchor you in the moment, reminding you that the power to act with intention is always within you. This simple, accessible tool is always ready to guide you back to your centre.

Though this book ends here, your journey continues.

One breath. One intention. One transformation at a time.

Thank you for walking this path with me.
With sincere best wishes,
Namita Jain

Acknowledgements

This book is born from a place of deep gratitude.

My first inspiration has always been my mother, born on April 7. The number 7 has carried a quiet magic throughout my life, and it felt only natural that *7 Breaths to Slimming* found its rhythm through her—a reminder that breath, like love, flows effortlessly across generations.

My heartfelt thanks to Geeta Gopalakrishnan, whose steadfast belief in the immense potential of this book encouraged me to begin writing it. Her encouragement was the catalyst that transformed an idea into a manuscript.

I am deeply grateful to the many business leaders, doctors, health experts and wellness mentors whose insights shaped the depth and accuracy of this work. Their wisdom added layers of clarity, science and practicality to every chapter. I would especially like to acknowledge the distinguished voices who endorsed this book. From the world of business: Kavita Singhania (Managing Director, Express Avenue), Atul Ruia (Chairman, The Phoenix Mills Ltd), Dr Abhay Firodia (Chairman, Force Motors Ltd), and Bharat Taparia (Chairman, Bombay Hospital Trust)—each of whom brought invaluable perspective and encouragement.

From sports and wellness, I am honoured to have the support of Saina Nehwal, Olympic medallist and former World No. 1 in badminton, and Subodh Tiwari, CEO of Kaivalyadhama, whose journeys embody discipline and wellbeing.

And from the field of medicine, I am grateful for the

guidance of Dr Ashwin Mehta (Cardiologist and Padma Bhushan Awardee), Dr Prasanna Shah (Gastroenterologist), Dr Shashank Shah (Bariatric and Metabolic Surgeon), Dr Dinshaw Pardiwala (Sports Orthopaedic Surgeon), and Dr Avya Bansal (Consultant Pulmonologist & Sleep Disorders Specialist).

Each of them contributed their voice, lending this book both credibility and strength.

My heartfelt gratitude to my friends and family for their unwavering support, patience and encouragement. Your faith held me steady through every step of this writing journey.

A sincere thank you to the MD and editorial team at Rupa Publications for their collaboration, clarity and commitment. Your guidance played an instrumental role in bringing this book to life with care and precision. A special shout-out to the dedicated editorial team—Aranya Dhar, Development Editor, and the wider Rupa team—for shaping this book so thoughtfully and bringing it to fruition. My deep appreciation also goes to Kapish Mehra, Managing Director, Rupa Publications, and Yamini Chowdhury, the dynamic Executive Editor, whose constant support and encouragement made it possible for this book to reach readers.

To everyone who touched this project—in ways big and small—thank you. This book carries your energy, your kindness, and your belief. If these pages make your wellness journey even a little lighter or more mindful, this effort has found its true purpose.